Ramayana *for* Children

Also for Young and New Readers

Ramayana *for* Children

Also for Young and New Readers

K.T. NARAYANAN

PRABHAT
PRAKASHAN

Published by
PRABHAT PRAKASHAN
4/19 Asaf Ali Road,
New Delhi-110002 (INDIA)
e-mail: prabhatbooks@gmail.com

ISBN 978-93-5521-757-8
RAMAYANA FOR CHILDREN
by K.T. Narayanan

Edition
First, 2023

Price
₹ 350 (Rupees Three Hundred Fifty Only)

Printed at
Nakshatra Art, Delhi

Author's Note

This book is based on *Valmiki Ramayana*. It has been written in a short and comprehensive form to make it easy to read and understandable for young and new readers. Anyone 10 years and above can go through Rama's journey with this book.

The story of Rama, Seetha and Hanuman is inspirational and provide many life lessons, even for this modern era. Ramayana means Rama's journey. The word *ayana* means travel in Sanskrit. Rama is famously called *Maryada Purushothama* where *maryada* denotes honour and righteousness while *Purushothama* means the supreme or the greatest man. Together, the phrase means 'the man who is supreme in honour and righteousness'. I hope that the story of Rama will enable everyone to live a life full of virtue, taking examples from his life as an ideal human. I would also like to mention the help provided by my beloved wife Ratnakumari Narayanan, and my daughters Amritha Dinesh and Anitha Sumit during the writing of this book.

This book is not based on *Adhyathma Ramayana* written by Vyasa muni.

Ramayana was originally written in verse and has seven chapters. Each chapter is called a *Kanda*. Originally it had six chapters and the seventh chapter was added later.

Chapter 1 is Bala Kanda; *bala* means child.

Chapter 2 is Ayodhya Kanda; Ayodhya, the kingdom of Rama or Dasaratha.

Chapter 3 is Aaranya Kanda; *aranya* means forest.

Chapter 4 is Kishkindha Kanda; Kishkindha, Vali/Sugreeva's kingdom.

Chapter 5 is Sundara Kanda; *sundara* means beautiful; this chapter is about Hanuman.

Chapter 6 is Yudha Kanda; *yudha* means war.

Chapter 7 is Uthara Kanda; *uthara* means answer.

– K.T. Narayanan

❑

How did the Concept of Writing Ramayana Take Place?

Once Narada muni visited Valmiki's ashram. Valmiki muni received him with all due respect and regards. An Ashram is a place where the *sanyasis,* or *munis* or *rishis* (ascetics) reside. They were simple, hut-like houses, generally in the forests. Valmiki muni asked Narada muni, "Who is the most noble person in the world? Who is the person with the following good qualities in the world? Knowledge, commanding power, brightness, truthfulness, smartness, a good character, love towards all living creatures, no anger, no ill-feeling towards others, does good governance of the people, and finally, has the grace of God."

Narada muni said, "There is a king named Rama in Ayodhya, who is the son of Dasaratha. He has all these above qualities."

Narada muni then left for heaven.

Valmiki muni along with his disciple, Bharadwaja muni, sat in meditation on the banks of the River Tamasa. During this time, a hunter came there and two birds started mating. The hunter shot the male bird and it died. Valmiki cursed the hunter, "You will never ever have mental peace in life." But later, he felt bad about his sudden anger.

Afterwards, Brahma visited Valmiki in his ashram. He informed Valmiki that he had created the anger in him, because that anger would lead him to a very good deed. This prompted Valmiki to start penance again. Due to the yogic power given to him by Brahma, he could visualise the complete life of Rama from his childhood. He thus wrote Ramayana which has 24,000 couplets in it. It was originally written in Sanskrit.

What lessons can we learn from Ramayana?

1. During student days, be proficient in all subjects including sports, music and all other available subjects, like Rama.
2. Learn to be obedient to your parents, teachers and elders. Be humble and bow to them. Touch their feet as a mark of respect and regards, in the appropriate circumstances.
3. How family members should love each other.
4. Devotion to duties, acquiring knowledge, a sweet and legible way of speaking and to be tough when the situation demands should be learned from Hanuman.
5. Seetha was very an ideal wife with good virtues. She was loyal to her husband and loving to her in-laws and all the other family members. She also had the courage to speak the truth infront of everyone without any fear.
6. Do not be arrogant or interested in grabbing wealth. Do not misbehave with women, or get pleasure in hurting others, like Ravana.
7. Learn the best administration from Rama who considers everyone equal. This was called Ramaraj which means equal opportunities for every citizen of the country.
8. Division of property equally to all family members before the last days of the life should be learnt from Rama, who made all his brothers and their children, kings and gave them their own kingdom to rule.

❑

Contents

Author's Note 5

How did the Concept of Writing Ramayana Take Place? 7

Chapter 1: Bala Kanda **11**

- Birth of the Princes 11
- Viswamitra's Visit 13

Chapter 2: Ayodhya Kanda **19**

- Dasaratha's Decision to Crown Rama as the King and Objection to it by Kaikeyi 20
- Travel of Rama, Lakshmana and Seetha to the Forest 22
- Bharadwaja Muni's Ashram 30
- Killing the Son of an Ascetic, His Curse and Dasaratha's Death 32

Chapter 3: Aaranya Kanda **42**

- Killing of Viradha and Visiting Sharabhanga Muni 42
- Travel to Panchavati, and Cutting the Nose and Ears of Shoorpanakha 45
- Ravana Abducting and Taking Seetha to Lanka 52

Chapter 4: Kishkindha Kanda **64**

- Meeting Hanuman and Sugreeva 64

- Killing of Vali and Crowning Sugreeva as the King 65
- Searching for Seetha 73

Chapter 5: Sundara Kanda **83**

- Hanuman Jumping to Lanka 83
- Finding Seetha 86
- Hanuman Entering Ravana's Palace and Burning the Lanka 93

Chapter 6: Yudha Kanda **104**

- Ravana in Anger, Walked Away 108
- Vibheeshana Meeting Rama 109
- Construction of Sethu Bridge 112
- War between Rama and Ravana 119
- Ravana's Death 141
- Rama Returning to Ayodhya 151

Chapter 7: Uthara Kanda **155**

- The Curses on Ravana 156
- Birth of Hanuman and His Blessings 159
- Ashwamedha Yagya 168
- Seetha Vanishing into the Earth 180
- The End of Rama's Life on Earth 182

Chapter 1
Bala Kanda

This chapter narrates Rama's story from his birth to his return to Ayodhya with his all brothers after his marriage to Seetha.

Ayodhya was the capital of the kingdom of Kosala on the banks of the river named Sarayu. Ayodhya was originally founded by Manu who came from the Suryavanshi or Ikshwaku dynasty. During those days, the city of Ayodhya was well-laid and glorious, and the people were very educated and cultured.

Once, a king named Dasaratha ruled the Ayodhya. The people were very happy and content during his rule. The great sage, Vasishta muni, was his adviser and he assisted him in his spiritual duties. The king had a number of ministers, one of whom was Sumanthra.

Birth of the Princes

King Dasaratha had three wives. Their names were Koushalya, Kaikeyi and Sumithra. He had a daughter named Shantha. He gave Shantha to his friend King Romapada who adopted her. Shantha was married to young Rishyashringa muni.

Sumanthra informed Dasaratha about the marriage of Shantha to Rishyashringa.

Dasaratha had no sons. For a king, it was necessary to have sons to keep up the continuity of the kingdom and transfer the power to the new prince.

Sumanthra told Dasaratha, "If we bring Rishyashringa to Ayodhya and conducts *yagya* which is called *Puthrakameshti*, there are good chances of having children." After hearing this, Dasaratha went to the palace of King Romapada. Dasaratha enjoyed the hospitality of the king for a few days. With King Romapada's permission, he then brought Rishyashringa and Shantha to Ayodhya.

The *Puthrakameshti yagya* was then conducted by Rishyashringa. A divine being emerged from the *yagya* with a golden bowl in his hand. He told Dasaratha, "I am the messenger of Brahma. Please accept this *payasam (kheer)* from the gods, Give it to your three wives. They will then deliver four sons."

Dasaratha gave one-fourth portion of the *payasam* to each of his wife Koushalya, Kaikeyi and Sumithra. The leftover portion of the payasam was again given to his third wife Sumithra They all became pregnant. Koushalya and Kaikeyi both gave birth to one son, while Sumithra gave birth to two sons.

Vasishta conducted the naming ceremony of the princes. Koushalya's son was named Rama, Kaikeyi's son Bharata, and Sumithra's two sons were named Lakshmana and Shatrughna.

The children started growing up. They received education from Vasishta muni. There were no schools during that period. The education was conducted by a sage in those days. It was called *gurukula* education at that time. They all received the knowledge of the Vedas, and were proficient in all kinds of weaponry and practices of administration. Although all the princes were wise and learned, Rama excelled in everything.

Rama and Lakshmana were devoted to each other, and Bharata and Shatrughna were close to each other, yet all the bothers loved one another equally . They grew into be young men. King Dasaratha started thinking about the marriage of the princes.

Viswamitra's Visit

One day, Viswamitra muni came to the palace of Dasaratha. Dasaratha received Viswamitra with all due respects and regards. Dasaratha told Viswamitra, "I am very happy about your visit to Ayodhya. I am feeling very honoured and blessed. Please tell me the purpose of your visit. I shall fulfil it, whatever it may be."

Viswamitra said, "I conduct *yagya* in the ashram. Two rakshasas named Subahu and Mareecha create obstructions to the *yaga*. They are cruel and get pleasure in harming and hurting others. These two rakshasas shower animals flesh and blood on the altar. I am unable to curse them as I should not show any anger. Rama will be able to kill them. Therefore, kindly send Rama with me. Please do not refuse to do so due to your love for your son Rama. If you send him, I shall confer my blessings on your son."

After hearing this, Dasaratha felt physically and mentally weak. He fell unconscious thinking of being separated from Rama. After regaining consciousness, he told Viswamitra, "Rama is very young. I can come with the army and kill those two rakshasas. Please do not force me to send Rama."

Viswamitra said, "These two rakshasas were sent by Ravana."

After hearing the name of Ravana, Dasaratha became very fearful. Dasaratha then said, "I will not send Rama in this case."

Viswamitra then became very angry. He told Dasaratha, "You had already promised to give me whatever I ask. Now refusing to keep that promise is very bad."

Vasishta arrived there at that time and asked Dasaratha to send Rama with Viswamitra. The king then sent for Rama and Lakshmana. Thereafter, Viswamitra left the palace with Rama and Lakshmana and started walking along the River Sarayu. After walking for a long time, they had a bath in the river. That night they slept on the banks of the river. In the morning, they continued walking along the Sarayu river and reached the joining place of the Sarayu and Ganga. They saw an ashram there. They took rest there.

The next day, the sage and the princes walked for a long time before they reached a big forest. Viswamithra said, "There is a wicked yakshini called Thadaka. Thadaka is the wife of a rakshasa called Sunda. Mareecha is their son. This wicked Thadaka harasses everyone. The people are afraid of her. So please kill Thadaka to save the people from her cruelty."

Rama agreed to follow the command of Viswamitra. Rama took his bow and pulled its string. The forest was filled with noise. On hearing the noise, Thadaka came there.

Thadaka had a monstrous and misshapen body. With her magical powers, she created a storm and started throwing big rocks at the princes. Rama cut off her hands while and Lakshmana cut off her nose and ears. She came running towards Rama with anger, but Rama killed her by showering many arrows on her.

Viswamitra then gifted Rama with many powerful weapons. After travelling furhter for some time, they finally reached Viswamitra's ashram. Viswamitra started a *yagya* (A type of ritual to seek God's grace by pouring some special items inside the fire and reciting Sanskrit mantras). Rama and Lakshmana kept a close watch for the arrival of Subahu and Mareecha. Subahu and Mareecha arrived there on the sixth day and started showering animal blood and flesh on the altar.

Rama told Lakshmana, "Their time of death has not come yet. Therefore, I will drive them away from here by showering continuous arrows on them."

Subahu and Mareecha ran away from there, fearing the deadly arrows of Rama. The munis in the ashram were very happy.

Viswamitra then asked Rama and Lakshmana to accompany him to Mithila, the kingdom of King Janaka along with few of his Brahmins. The king was conducting a sacrifice in Mithila. King Janaka had a divine bow and arrow there. This was given by Lord Shiva to King Devavratha, an ancestor of the king of Mithila. It was securely kept there.

On the way to Mithila, they saw an ashram which was uninhabited. Rama asked Viswamitra about the ashram. Viswamitra said, "It was the ashram of Gouthama muni and his wife Ahalya. One day, when Gouthama was not in the ashram, Indra took the form of Gouthama and mated with Ahalya. Gouthama came to know about it and cursed Ahalya and Ahalya became a rock. He also said that when Rama will come to the forest and place his feet on Ahaly, then she would regain her human form."

Viswamitra with Rama and Lakshmana went to the ashram. Rama and Lakshmana saw Ahalya because of her yogic powers. Ahalya touched Rama's feet and regained her original human form. Gouthama muni came at that time, welcomed and accepted Ahalya again. After bowing to Rama and Lakshmana, he left the ashram with Ahalya.

Viswamithra and the princes then reached Mithila. King Janaka received them with due honour. He asked Viswamitra about the two persons accompanying him. Viswamitra said, "They are Rama and Lakshmana, sons of the Ayodhya king, Dasaratha. I had brought them to my ashram where my *yagya* was continuously disturbed by two rakshasas Subahu and Mareecha. They have performed their duty. We have come here to see the divine bow and arrow that is in your family's possession."

Janaka said, "The divine weapon was given to Devavratha, one of our ancestor by Lord Shiva as a gift. Once when I was ploughing the land where a *yagya* was performed, I got a baby girl from the furrow. I gave her thc name Seetha. I took her as my adopted daughter and brought her up.

She has now reached the age of marriage. Many kings came here asking to marry her. But Seetha is very special. She wants a husband who is noble, a courageous warrior and proficient in weaponry."

Viswamitra asked Janaka, "What type of a courageous warrior does she expect?" Janaka said, "The first person who can lift the bow and string it, will be her husband. All the kings who came were not able to even lift or move the bow."

Janaka invited Rama and showed him the bow and arrow. So far nobody was able to even move it. Rama looked at the bow and placed his left hand on the bow. Rama then effortlessly, lifted the bow with his left hand in the presence of all people. He was able to strung the bow easily but due to his mighty strength, the bow broke with a thunderous noise. All the people around were afraid after hearing this noise.

Janaka then decided to arrange the marriage of Rama and Seetha. He sent his messengers to Ayodhya to inform King Dasaratha about the great deed done by Rama and his impending marriage to Seetha. Dasaratha in consultation with Vasishta decided to go to Mithila with all family members. Janaka received them all with due respect and regards.

Viswamitra then requested Janaka to give his daughter Urmila, in marriage to Lakshmana. The marriage of Rama and Lakshmana was to be conducted together. Later, Vasishta and Viswamitra requested Janaka to give Mandavi and Shruthikeerthi, the daughters of King Kushadvaja, King Janaka's brother, in marriage to Bharata and Shatrughna. Janaka happily agreed to all marriage proposals. After three days, the marriage of all four sons of Dasaratha was conducted. The first marriage was that of Rama and Seetha. The marriage of Lakshmana and Urmila was conducted next. After that the marriages of Bharata and Mandavi and Shatrughna and Shruthikeerthi were conducted.

The next day, Viswamitra left for the Himalayan mountains and Dasaratha left for Ayodhya with all his family members along with Vasishta. On their way home, they saw many deers running frightened and heard the screeching of birds.

"Does this indicate a bad omen?" asked Viswamitra.

Vasishta replied, "It does indicate danger, but all will be fine."

A heavy wind started blowing after that. The trees were uprooted and there was dust flying all around. Parashurama appeared in front of them in a fearful form. There was an axe on his right shoulder, an arrow in his left hand and a bow in his right hand. After destroying the Kshatriyas (king's family) 21 times, he was about to start meditation to control his anger. He told Rama with anger, "You are a great person who broke the bow of Lord Shiva. I have a bow and arrow with me which is more powerful than that and it was given to me by the Lord Vishnu. If you have the capacity to use this bow by tying its string and fight with me, I will admit that there is an opponent equal to me."

Dasaratha was terribly afraid after hearing this.

Parashurama continued, "Once the gods asked Brahma which was the greater bow. Brahma started a war between Lord Shiva and Vishnu. Lord Vishnu broke the string of Lord Shiva's bow and won the battle. Lord Shiva gave his bow and arrow to Devavratha while Lord Vishnu gave his bow and arrow to my great-grandfather Hrichika muni. I was going to the Himalayas for meditation, when I came to know about your breaking of the bow given by Lord Shiva. If you are brave enough, take this bow and arrow and fight with me."

Rama took the bow and arrow from Parashurama and strung the bow and placed an arrow in it. Rama then told Parashurama, "I can't kill you since you are a Brahmin. However, with this arrow, I will destroy all the powers you have so far acquired by meditation."

Parashurama's pride vanished and he humbly said to Rama, "You are Vishnu himself and therefore I do not feel bad about losing the battle to you."

Parashurama then left for the Mahendragiri Mountain. Rama gave this divine bow and arrow to the god Varuna.

The four sons of Dasaratha with their wives soon reached Ayodhya. They lived in happiness for some time. One day, King Yudhajith came to Ayodhya. He was the maternal uncle of Bharata. He took Bharata and Shatrughna to his Kekeya kingdom to stay there for some time.

Seetha was an embodiment of Lakshmi Devi. She was a divine beauty. The relationship between Rama and Seetha was like that between Lord Vishnu and Lakshmi Devi.

❑

Chapter 2
Ayodhya Kanda

This chapter starts from Dasaratha's decision to make Rama the king and to honour the two promises Dasaratha had given to Kaikeyi. Accordingly Rama, Seetha and Lakshmana leave for the forest to stay there for 14 years. Rama meets Athri muni in the forest and goes to the Dandaka Forest.

Bharata and Shatrughna stayed in their maternal uncle's house for some time. Rama became the favourite and most liked prince of Ayodhya. Dasaratha too loved him very much. Rama was affectionate to all, and had regard for God-loving people, wise people and Brahmins. He loved all the people of Ayodhya and they too loved him. He was very good in governance principles and in war tactics and strategies.

Dasaratha had become old. He therefore summoned all his ministers and important persons including Vasishta muni to the court. He told them that he had decided to hand over the throne to Rama and crown him as the king. He asked his minister Sumanthra to start making arrangements for the crowning ceremony of Rama. All the people in Ayodhya came to know about this and were overjoyed and thrilled to hear about the crowning ceremony. All the houses were decorated and flower garlands adorned the streets. Manthara came to know about the crowning of Rama. Manthara was Kaikeyi's maid.

Dasaratha's Decision to Crown Rama as the King and Objection to it by Kaikeyi

Manthara went to Kaikeyi and told her, "You are in danger, Kaikeyi. Did you not know that Rama is going to be made king of Ayodhya? That too when your children were sent away from here!"

Kaikeyi was very happy to know this news. Manthara was angry when she saw that Kaikeyi was happy to know this news. She told Kaikeyi, "You are a fool. Dasaratha had given you two promises when you saved his life during the war that the asuras had waged against Indra. You should now ask him to keep those two promises and ask for the things that you want from him. You should remove all your gold ornaments and royal dresses, wear ordinary dresses, go to the *kopagriha* (room of rage) and lie down on the ground weeping. Dasaratha loves you very much and he will not be able to see your sadness. When he comes to you, ask him to honour those two promises. First one should be to make Bharata the king and the second that Rama should be exiled to the forest for 14 years. You should be very firm about this. If he does not agree to this, you should say that you will drink poison and die."

Kaikeyi accordingly agreed for this. She removed all her gold ornaments and royal dresses and wore an ordinary dress. She then went to the *kopagriha* and lay there pretending to be sad and angry.

The preparation for the crowning ceremony of Rama was almost over by that time. After that, Dasaratha came to the palace. He went to see Kaikeyi, his favourite wife. She was not in her palace chambers. He finally saw her in the *kopagriha*, lying on the floor without any gold ornaments and wearing a soiled dress. She was crying. Dasaratha lovingly touched her face and asked her what had happened. "Did anybody insult you or get angry with you?"

Kaikeyi said, "Nobody has done anything to me. First you promise me that you will honour those two promises you had made to me."

Dasaratha told Kaikeyi, "I shall be happy to honour my promises but tell me what they are."

Then Kaikeyi said, "You had made two promises to me during the war with Indra, when I took you away from the battlefield when you were injured and saved your life. I am now asking you to keep those two promises. I am now going to ask those two things from you. First, instead of Rama, Bharata should be crowned as the king. Second one is that Rama should be exiled to the forest for 14 years."

After hearing this, Dasaratha became very emotional and angry and then be fell unconscious. After regaining consciousness, he asked Kaikeyi why she was behaving in such a manner and showing such cruelty to him.

Dasaratha said, "I can give up anything but not Rama." After that Dasaratha fell at Kaikeyi's feet and told her, "I can make Bharata king. But do not insist on sending Rama to the forest." Dasaratha then cried.

Kaikeyi was not moved by these words. She was firm in her demands that Dasaratha keep the two promises. Kaikeyi said, "You are morally obliged and as a king, responsible to keep your promises. If you do not keep them, I will drink poison and die."

Dasaratha again became unconscious after hearing this. He spent the night there. The next day, the king woke up in the morning by the royal musicians. For a king would be woken up with music and musical instruments. Dasaratha sent them back. Kaikeyi again reminded Dasaratha about the two promises he had made. "If you believe in truth and morality, ensure that the promises are kept. You can call Rama and inform him all about this."

Travel of Rama, Lakshmana and Seetha to the Forest

At the same time, Vasishta and his disciples were busy in the preparation of Rama's crowning ceremony. Vasishta asked Sumanthra, "Inform Dasaratha that the time for the coronation of Rama is near."

Sumanthra reached Dasaratha's royal chamber and as was the custom, praised the king and informed him about the message of Vasishta. Dasaratha became very angry and asked Sumanthra to leave the place. Seeing this, Kaikeyi told Sumanthra, "The king did not sleep well yesterday. That is why he is angry. You go and bring Rama here."

Sumanthra thought that Dasaratha was summoning Rama to discuss the crowning ceremony.

The preparation for the crowning ceremony had begun with the preparation of the *homa kund* (A fire place to conduct marriage). The actual ceremony had not started. Yet Sumanthra informed Rama about Dasaratha's wish to see him. Rama thought that his father was summoning him in relation to his installation as the regent. He told this to Seetha. Seetha happily sent him, praying to the various gods to bless him.

Rama then went to his father's chambers to see him. He saw his father sitting on a couch with Kaikeyi. Rama understood the sadness and anxiousness of his father from his facial expressions. Rama fell at their feet. Dasaratha had no courage to look at the face of Rama. He just muttered, "Rama, Rama …" his eyes were full of tears.

Rama asked Kaikeyi, "What happened to Father? He always used to be happy while seeing me. Did I hurt him in any way?"

Kaikeyi said, "Nothing has happened to him. He had made two promises to me when I saved him from the battlefield. I have now asked him to honour those two promises. He felt mentally disturbed when I asked for them. If you assure me that you will help your father to keep those promises, I will tell you what they are."

Rama said, "Believe me and tell me what they are. I am prepared to carry them out. I will do everything that he desires to protect his name and fame."

Kaikeyi said, "The first one is that Bharata should be made king in your place. Second one is that you should live for 14 years in the Dandaka Forest as an ascetic and wear clothes made of leaves and deerskin."

Rama did not show any signs of being upset after he heard this. He told Kaikeyi, "I shall do as you wish, happily. I will now go to the forest immediately. You can send messengers to Bharata and make him the king."

Kaikeyi was very happy. She immediately sent messengers to summon Bharata. After hearing all this, Dasaratha became unconscious again.

Rama came out of the royal chamber. Lakshmana was standing outside, he had overheard the whole conversation. His eyes were filled with tears and anger. Rama then went to his mother, Koushalya's chamber to inform her about all the new developments. Koushalya was worshipping Lord Vishnu at that time. She told Rama, "I am very happy to hear that you are going to be the king of the kingdom of Kosala."

Rama told Koushalya calmly, "Please listen carefully to what I have to say. Do not lose your mental control. Father had made two promises to mother Kaikeyi. Father had agreed to keep up those promises and according to that, Bharata will be crowned as the king in my place and I should stay for 14 years in the forest like an ascetic. I have to leave for the forest now."

Koushalya fell down in shock on hearing this. Rama helped his mother up and made her rest on the couch. Koushalya then told Rama, "This is the worst and unluckiest thing that has ever happened to me. It is better to die rather than hear this."

Lakshmana lost his cool on listening to all this. Lakshmana told Koushalya, "Let us conduct the crowning ceremony of Rama, before all the people come to know about the decision of Father to make Bharata the king. Father's decision was wrong. I owe everything only to Rama and not to anybody else."

Koushalya then told Rama, "Let Bharata be the king. But you should not go to the forest. If you go to the forest, I will starve and die."

Then Rama said, "I have to obey Father's order and can't go against it." Rama told Lakshmana, "Lakshmana, please control your anger. Do not take over the kingdom by force. I have to go to the forest and stay there for 14 years as desired by Father. I plead with both of you to not make any obstruction in it. If Bharata becomes the king, everything will become all right. Let us not blame anybody. Let us consider it as our fate."

However, Lakshmana was still not calm, but angry. Rama talked to Lakshmana and pacified him. Then Koushalya told

Rama to take her also to the forest. Rama then told Koushalya, "If you do that, Father may die due to mental agony. You should not leave Father and come with me. You must stay with him as your place is beside him. I will come back after 14 years."

Koushalya finally agreed with Rama. She gave permission to Rama to go to the forest and also blessed him. Rama fell at the feet of his mother and sought her blessings and left the place. He went to his chambers in the palace.

Seetha was eagerly waiting there to see Rama. Seeing Rama's face which was not cheerful and bright as usual, she was filled with fear. She then asked him, "What happened to you?" Without any hesitation, Rama explained all the incidents that had taken place including the two promises that Dasaratha had made to Kaikeyi and accordingly, the decision of crowning Bharata and Rama's 14 years' stay in the forest. Rama said, "I have to obey Father's instruction and help him to keep his promises. You therefore stay here."

Seetha was angry on hearing his words and said emotionally, "Your advice is not correct. Whatever may be the difficulty of the husband, the wife has to be with him sharing his sorrows and pain. I will therefore come with you. There is no change in that. I am prepared to stay in the forest and undergo any suffering. I will not get physically or mentally shattered. You are everything for me. If you will not listen to me, I will drink poison and die."

Seetha cried so much that she fell unconscious. Rama held her in his arms and spoke tenderly to her, "If you are resolved to come with me, then do so."

Rama told her to give as alms, all her gold ornaments and clothes to Brahmins. Lakshmana fell at Rama's feet and requested him to allow him also to accompany him to the forest. Rama told him to remain there to take care of their mothers. Lakshmana did not agree to this. Lakshmana said, "I will come to help you in all matters. I will gather food for you and show you the way. Bharata will take care of all our mothers."

Rama agreed to take Lakshmana too along with him. Rama asked Lakshmana to carry with him the divine bow of King Janaka with the arrows and swords presented to him by King Janaka. Lakshmana brought the weapons. Rama gave away all his belongings as alms to good Brahmins, dependents, relatives and poor people. Rama, Seetha and Lakshmana then went to Dasaratha's chamber. They asked Sumanthra to announce their arrival to the king. Dasaratha on seeing Rama, ran to embrace him but fell unconscious.

Rama helped his father up and made him lie down on the couch. Dasaratha opened his eyes. Rama told Dasaratha, "I am leaving for the forest along with Seetha and Lakshmana. Please grant your permission for that. I tried my best to dissuade them from coming with me, but in vain. They are coming with me."

Dasaratha then told Rama, "Put me in the prison and take over the palace and become the king. I do not now have any desire to rule the country and to enjoy the kingly life happily."

Hearing his father's words, Rama just said, "Dear Father, do not be upset. I shall go away for 14 years and then come back to take care of you."

Dasaratha then gave them permission to leave and requested Rama to stay one day with him. Rama said, "I have to leave now only to keep the promises and it is my duty too." Dasaratha lovingly hugged Rama.

Sumanthra filled with anger, scolded Kaikeyi with harsh words. He said, "You are a cruel woman, to send Rama to the forest. This will lead to the destruction of the family and the death of your husband. It is the tradition to make the eldest son the king." Kaikeyi was not at all moved by his words, and remained standing without any change of heart. Dasaratha then instructed Sumanthra to send army men and servants with weapons and wealth to accompany Rama. Kaikeyi objected to this too. "Rama should go empty-handed," she said. Kaikeyi then went to her room and came out with clothes of bark for Rama, Seetha and Lakshmana. Rama and Lakshmana wore those dresses. Tears were dripping from Seetha's eyes due to sorrow and the thought of wearing such clothes. Rama helped her by fastening the robe of bark over her saree.

Vasishta muni could not control himself on seeing all this. He told Kaikeyi, "All the people of Ayodhya will leave along with Rama. You are an extremely bad and devilish woman. You and Bharata will rule an empty Ayodhya."

After seeing Rama, Lakshmana and Seetha dressed in the simple garments of bark, the people present in the palace became angry with Dasaratha and cursed him with abusive words. Dasaratha felt that death was better than living like this. He asked Sumanthra, "Sumanthra, bring the chariot and escort Rama to the forest."

Koushalya then told Seetha, "You should not hate Rama. Let him always be your caring and loving husband." Seetha humbly told Koushalya, "I will obey you. I know the duty a wife has towards her husband. I will honour and serve him."

Rama, Seetha and Lakshmana then fell at the feet of Dasaratha and Koushalya, and showed their respect and regards for them. Lakshmana then fell at the feet of his mother Sumithra. Sumithra blessed him and said that she was happy that Lakshmana was accompanying Rama to the forest.

By now, Sumanthra had arrived with the chariot. Rama, Seetha and Lakshmana mounted the chariot and they started their journey to the forest. The people of Ayodhya gathered on the streets to watch their beloved princes and princess leave. "Sumanthra, please drive slowly so that we can see their faces for as long as possible", said Dasaratha as he also came along with the crowd of people and accompanied the chariot. Rama instructed Sumanthra to drive the chariot fast. Sumanthra was confused and did not know what to do. Rama again told Sumanthra to drive fast and he drove the chariot fast, the dust kicked up by the wheels.

Dasaratha stricken with grief, fell to the earth. Koushalya and Kaikeyi rushed to help him up. Dasaratha then told Kaikeyi, "You wicked queen, do not touch me. You are no longer my wife."

On the way back to the palace, Dasaratha observed that all the streets and shops were deserted. The people in Ayodhya were in mourning. Dasaratha told Koushalya to take him to her chambers. Dasaratha did not sleep well that night. He could sleep only after he held Koushalya's hand. Sumithra came to the chambers and consoled Koushalya. "Rama will not have any difficulty when both Lakshmana and Seetha are with him. Rama is not an ordinary person. You should consider him as an embodiment of God. He will definitely come back. Please do not be sad."

All the people of Ayodhya had accompanied Rama to the forest. Rama asked all of them to go back. "My father has made Bharata the king. You must go back and obey him. He will rule you in my absence. Now let me keep my promise."

Rama, Lakshmana and Seetha got down from the chariot and sent back the chariot and the people. They started walking. Soon, they reached the banks of the Tamasa River. Dusk was approaching. Sumanthra and Lakshmana collected some leaves and made a bed for Rama to sleep on. Rama and Seetha slept there on the bed. Sumanthra and Lakshmana stayed awake, guarding the couple.

On waking up, Rama saw the people, who had come along with him, sleeping on the ground. Rama told Sumanthra to take them away from this place before the people got up. They all got onto the chariot and crossed the river to the other side. When the people got up, they did not see Rama, Lakshmana and Seetha. They returned to Ayodhya with sorrow and a heavy heart. They all blamed Kaikeyi for everything that had happened. The city of

Ayodhya looked deserted and still. Very few shops were open. All the people were unhappy.

Rama and the others soon reached the southern border of Kosala. After crossing the border, Rama folded his hands and bowed to his city. After travelling for some time, they reached the banks of the Ganga River. They halted their journey there and rested under the foot of an ingudi tree. They reached the place called Nishada. The king of that place was Guha, who was a friend of Rama. Guha arrived there after knowing the news of the arrival of Dasaratha's sons and hugged Rama. He felt very sad on seeing them dressed in clothes of bark. He welcomed Rama to his city, Shringaverapura and told him, "You are my guest." Guha had brought dishes of delicious food, beds and flowers for puja. "Offering flowers is a method of praying to God."

Rama was very happy and hugged Guha and told him, "I can only receive all these items in my heart. According to the vow I have taken, during my stay in the forest, I am not in a position to use or accept these." That day Rama and Seetha slept below a tree. Lakshmana and Guha were on guard.

Guha arranged a boat for them the next day to cross the River Ganga. Rama told Sumanthra to go back to Ayodhya and serve his father patiently and with devotion. Sumanthra asked Rama's permission to accompany him but Rama did not agree. Rama reminded Sumanthra, "We will come back to Ayodhya after 14 years. Once Bharata is made king, serve him well and ask him to honour my father and my mothers." Then Sumanthra went back to Ayodhya.

Rama then told Guha, "We must take leave of you too now." Rama, Lakshmana and Seetha climbed into the boat and reached the southern shore. Then they got out of the boat and walked on foot. Lakshmana walked in front, Seetha in the middle and Rama behind. Rama again told Lakshmana to go back and take care of their mothers and father. Lakshmana did not agree. They decided to take rest below a tree. Seetha slept on the while Rama and Lakshmana guarded her.

Bharadwaja Muni's Ashram

The next day, they rose and walked through the forest till they reached the ashram of Bharadwaja muni and waited respectfully in front of the ashram. A disciple of the muni greeted them and took them inside the ashram. Rama bowed to the muni and explained about the circumstances that had led them there. The muni received them graciously and offered them roots and fruits as food. After he had shown them a place where they could rest, the muni told Rama, "You are welcome to stay here for 14 years. My disciples are there to take care of all of you. You will not feel any inconvenience."

Rama then told Bharadwaja, "If we stay here, the people from Ayodhya will soon come to know. Then they will start coming to see us. Please therefore tell us a place where we can stay and will feel happy, content and can get privacy."

Bharadwaja suggested a place which was about ten *yojanas* (yojana= 2.4 km) from there. "Ten *yojanas* from here, you will find a big tree (a special type of tree). That means you have reached a place called Chitrakoot. It is a very beautiful place, filled with fruits and flowers. Animals wander in the forests which is abound with streams and waterfalls. You can happily stay there."

They spent that night in Bharadwaja muni's ashram.

The next day with the blessings and good wishes of the muni, they left the ashram and proceeded in the direction as told by the muni. They soon reached the banks of the Yamuna River. Rama and Lakshmana made a raft out of the bamboo and *kusha* grass. Then, they got on the raft and reached the other side of the river. On the opposite side, they saw a mighty fig tree as told by the muni, which was the indication of the location of Chitrakoot.

After resting that night, they started their journey again the next morning. Rama pointed out to Seetha the beautiful trees and flowers on the way. They finally reached Chitrakoot, a beautiful place full of fruits, flowers and pools filled with pure water. Soon they saw Valmiki muni's ashram. The muni welcomed them warmly. He was waiting for their arrival. He asked them to stay there.

Rama said, "Lakshmana, let us stay here. Make a hut for us to stay." Lakshmana then chopped some wood and constructed a hut with wooden walls and a ceiling with grass. Rama had a bath and then he prayed to God and offered fruits and flowers. After chanting some *mantras*, Rama and Seetha entered the house. Meanwhile, Guha had found out the place where Rama, Lakshmana and Seetha were staying. He sent this information to Sumanthra. Sumanthra returned to Ayodhya only after getting this message.

Ayodhya appeared deserted. The streets were silent and not many people were around. The people of Ayodhya soon came to know about the arrival of Sumanthra. They asked him about Rama, Lakshmana and Seetha. Sumanthra told them that he had taken them to the banks of the Ganga River. Sumanthra then reached the palace to see King Dasaratha. When Sumanthra started talking about Rama, Dasaratha became unconscious due to extreme sadness and emotional distress. He fell down before Sumanthra and Koushalya could reach him. Koushalya too was overcome with distress and fell to the floor senseless.

Dasaratha soon regained consciousness and asked Sumanthra about what all had happened after he had left Ayodhya. "O Sumanthra, how are Rama and Lakshmana? Where will they stay? What will they eat? Tell me everything."

Sumanthra then told Dasaratha everything. "Before taking my leave, he told me to go back to Ayodhya and serve you well. He told me to make Bharata the king and crown him immediately. He also asked Bharata to take care of all the mothers impartially and lovingly."

Koushalya then vent her fury on Dasaratha. "You are responsible for all this. Your love for Kaikeyi was the cause for everything. How will Rama, Lakshmana and Seetha live in the forest eating only fruits and roots? How will they live and survive in the dense forest where all wild animals roam? What is the guarantee that Bharata will give the kingdom back to Rama when he comes back after 14 years? Will Rama be ready to take back the kingdom from Bharata?"

Killing the Son of an Ascetic, His Curse and Dasaratha's Death

Dasaratha then narrated an incident when he was young. "I had the ability and training to send the arrows to a place from where sound emanates; my arrow would reach and strike the object making the sound. One night, I was hunting near the banks of the Sarayu River, when I heard the sound of an elephant drinking water. I sent my arrow towards that sound when I heard the sound of a man shouting in pain. 'I am the son of an ascetic. Who has attacked me with such cruelty?' I went there immediately

and saw a young man who had fallen on the ground. The boy said, 'I had came here to fetch water for my blind parents. They are waiting for me for the water. You have killed not only me but also my blind parents. Please pull the arrow from my body, I can't bear the pain. If you remove the arrow from my body, I will die.' The moment I removed the arrow the young man breathed his last."

Dasaratha continued, "I then filled water in a pot and went with that to the ailing blind parents of the boy. I told them that I had killed their son by mistaking the sound of his filling the pitcher for that of an elephant.

The father said, 'Since you have admitted your mistake, I am not cursing you. Take us to our son's side.' They conducted all the required rituals after death including preparation of the funeral pyre. After that, the father said, 'You will also suffer similar sadness like us due to your son.' Both the parents jumped into the burning fire of cremation and went to heaven."

King Dasaratha was so distressed that he passed away in his sleep that night. The next day in the morning, the royal musicians went to wake up the king. They saw that the king was no more. They cried loudly. Koushalya and Sumithra woke up on hearing the cries. They cried at the loss of their husband. The cremation of the king could not be conducted without the presence of his son/sons. The body was therefore kept in oil, in a wooden trough to prevent deterioration of the dead body.

Vasishta muni, Markandeya muni, Kashyapa muni, Gouthama muni and other Brahmins decided that somebody had to be crowned king immediately. It had been already decided to make Bharata the king. They therefore sent emissaries to bring Bharata and Shatrughna as their presence was essential in Ayodhya. Meanwhile, Bharata had a dream which indicated that either his father or brother would die. While he was telling Shatrughna his dream, the emissaries from Ayodhya came and asked them to leave immediately for Ayodhya. They did not inform Bharata about the death of Dasaratha.

After a journey of seven days, they reached Ayodhya. Bharata noticed that all the people looked sad and the lanes are lonely and deserted. He first went to his father's chamber in the palace. He could not see his father. He then went to Kaikeyi. Kaikeyi lovingly patted Bharata. He asked his mother about his father and the wretched state Ayodhya was in. Kaikeyi calmly told Bharata that King Dasaratha was dead.

Bharata asked Kaikeyi, "How did he die? Was there any special message for me? Please therefore send an emissary to Rama to inform him about my coming here."

Kaikeyi then said, "Rama, Lakshmana and Seetha are not here. They have gone to the forest to stay there for 14 years. Your father passed away due to sadness of staying away from Rama. He was crying, calling the names of all three."

Bharata then asked his mother, "Why was Rama sent to the forest? What crime did he commit?"

Kaikeyi then explained to Bharata what all had happened. The decision of his father to crown Rama as king, the two promises his father had vowed to her and her asking him to keep the promises; one to make Bharata as king and the other to send Rama to the forest for 14 years. "I did all these exclusively for your sake. Do the required cremation ceremony of your father and then get crowned yourself and become the king of Ayodhya."

Bharata became angry after hearing all this. He then said, "You are a wretched woman. You have indirectly killed him. Your desires will not get fulfilled. I will go to the forest and bring Rama. I will give the kingdom to my deserving elder brother. I will serve under him." Bharata then fell unconscious due to anger and distress. When he recovered, he summoned the ministers. Bharata told them, "I will serve under Rama. I am not a party to my mother's crooked plan of ousting Rama from the kingdom."

Kaikeyi lost all hope and was very sad. Bharata and Shatrughna then went to see Koushalya. Koushalya asked Bharata, "Have you now come here to enjoy the kingdom? Was it your desire also?"

Bharata was very sad after hearing this from mother Koushalya and could not utter a word and became speechless and then he said, " All these are the crooked plans of my mother. I am not involved in that crooked plan. I love Rama very much and will always serve Rama."

Koushalya's doubts about Bharata vanished after hearing his words. She consoled Bharata. Vasishta muni then advised Bharata to do the last rites for the king. King Dasaratha's body was removed from the oil and then adorned with precious gems. The necessary customs, procedures and rituals were followed and the body was placed on the pyre. The cremated ashes were thrown in the River Sarayu and allowed to flow with the water as per normal custom.

Bharata fell on the floor crying. "O Father, why did you leave me alone and go? My brother Rama has gone away for 14 years. Where have you gone brother, leaving mother Koushalya alone?"

Vasishta muni consoled both Bharata and Shatrughna. At that moment, Manthara arrived at the gates of the palace. The guards dragged her in front of Shatrughna and said, "She is the evil lady who persuaded Kaikeyi to send Rama to the forest. This wicked lady is also the cause of Dasaratha's death." Shatrughna threw Manthara on the floor and dragged her. The women servants ran away from there after seeing the anger of Shatrughna. Trembling with fear, Manthra sought refuge with Bharata.

Bharata said, "Shatrughna, we must not harm women." Shatrughna then released Manthara.

The next day, the musicians came to wake up Bharata in the morning. Bharata told them, "I am not the king of Ayodhya."

Vasishta muni reached the palace and gave a message to all ministers, army officials, and very important citizens to come to the palace. Vasishta muni told Bharata, "All formalities are ready for your crowning ceremony and the people are waiting for you."

Bharata said, "The eldest son should be made the king. I am not therefore ready to be the king. I am going to the forest to bring back Rama. Ask the army to make a road to go to the forest."

The people felt sad about Bharata's decision and at the same time they felt proud too. The ministers sent some people to construct a road from Ayodhya to the shores of the River Ganga and it was done in a short period.

The next day Sumanthra came with the chariot for Bharata. The army men followed them in sixty thousand chariots. Koushalya, Sumithra and Kaikeyi accompanied them in another chariot. After travelling a considerable distance, they reached the banks of the River Ganga. Guha felt suspicious after he saw the army of men and chariots.

"Have they come here to attack Rama?", Guha thought to himself. He then went and met Bharata with many gifts to know the purpose of his visit. Sumanthra, after seeing Guha told Bharata about the good and warm relation Rama had with Guha. Guha, the king of the Nishada kingdom received Bharata with all courtesy expected of a host and friend and promised all the required help to him. Bharata asked him the location of Bharadwaja muni's ashram and how to go there. Guha agreed to take them there, but wanted to know the real purpose of his coming here with the army.

Bharata said, "I feel sad on hearing this from you. I have come here to persuade Rama to come back to Ayodhya and request him to become the king and take over the Ayodhya kingdom."

Guha was now totally convinced about Bharata's good intention. It became dark and the night approached. Guha then told Bharata of how Rama and Seetha had slept here on a bed made of leaves and how he and Lakshmana had kept a watch on them through the night. He also said that on the next day, Rama, Seetha and Lakshmana had worn clothes made of bark and went to the other side of the river. After hearing this, Bharata had doubts whether Rama would come back to Ayodhya.

The next day, Guha arranged boats so that they could all cross the River Ganga. The army men, people and the horses went in big boats; the elephants swam to the other side of the Ganga with them. Bharata was now dressed in clothes of bark. Guha showed them to Bharadwaja muni's ashram. It was about seven kms away from there. The army men camped there. Bharata along with Vasishta muni went to Bharadwaja's ashram. Bharadwaja muni got up and welcomed Vasishta muni. After greeting them and receiving them courteously, Bharadwaja muni asked, "Prince, please clearly tell me the purpose of your visit. I hope that you have not come here to harm Rama."

Bharata then said, "Your words have saddened me." With tears in his eyes, he said, "The purpose of my visit is to take Rama back and persuade and request him to be the king and take over the kingdom."

Bharadwaja then told Bharata, "With my meditative power, I already knew everything about you. However, I wanted to hear it from you. You can take rest here today and then go to Chitrakoot tomorrow." The muni then arranged food for all of them including the army.

Bharata started his journey the next day with his mothers. He introduced Koushalya, Kaikeyi and Sumitra to Bharadwaja muni. "My mother Kaikeyi is the one to blame for all this."

Bharadwaja muni then told Bharata not to blame his mother. "There is a good, very desirable unknown reason behind all this. The role of your mother is only a part of it." After bowing to the muni, they started their journey to Chitrakoot with the army. They saw some smoke emanating from a distance. Bharata asked the army to wait there and Bharata, Shatrughna and Vasishta muni with some other people went in that direction.

Rama and Seetha seated on a rock, were enjoying the beauty of nature. Rama was pointing out to Seetha the animals, flowers, trees and the birds in that area. Suddenly, he also saw the dust rising in the sky due to the arrival of an army of men. The animals too fled in fear on hearing the din created by the nearing army. Lakshmana climbed on top of a tree and saw an army with chariots, horses and elephants. "Rama, Bharata is coming with his army . I am sure he is planning to kill us both. Let us hide Seetha in a cave, climb on a hilltop and get ready to face the army. I am ready to kill Bharata and the entire army."

Rama then told Lakshmana, "He may be coming to give back the kingdom to me. If you want to take over the kingdom by defeating Bharata, I will tell Bharata to hand over the kingdom in a peaceful way."

Rama then returned to the ashram with Lakshmana and Seetha. Bharata, Shatrughna and Guha after noticing smoke rising from the ashram, walked towards that area. Bharata requested Vasishta to bring his mothers to the ashram. Finally they reached Rama's ashram.

Bharata after seeing Rama in clothes of deerskin and bark, said with tears in the eyes, "My heart breaks after seeing you in these clothes. You are suffering, leaving the kingly luxurious life because of me." Bharata then fell at Rama's feet, unable to speak because of grief.

Rama hugged Bharata. Rama then asked Bharata, "Why did you come here instead of taking care of Father? Tell me the news about our mothers and the people of Ayodhya. I hope you have been able to rule the kingdom well." Rama then lectured to Bharata on how to rule a country with proper justice and equality to all. He also gave him proper advice on how to choose ministers and friends. Rama had noticed that Bharata was dressed in garments of bark and thought that he might have done it due to his love for him.

Bharata after hearing all this said, "I am not responsible for the wicked actions of my mother and am not part of it. Please come back to Ayodhya and take over the kingdom. All the people of Ayodhya are depressed and not happy in your absence." He then fell at Rama's feet with the request to come back.

Rama lifted him up and lovingly told him, "I know that you are not a party in sending me to the forest. Do not blame your mother or father for that. You go back to Ayodhya, get yourself crowned and take over the kingdom. I will remain in the forest for 14 years as per Father's wish and will come back to Ayodhya."

Bharata then said, "When the elder brother is living, nobody including me has the right to become the king. Our father has passed away, due to grief. Please come back to Ayodhya and take over the kingdom."

Rama became unconscious after hearing the news of the death of his father. Seetha, Bharata and Lakshmana sprinkled water on Rama's face and he then got up. He was extremely sad about the death of his father. Rama then told Bharata that he would not come back to Ayodhya now. The brothers and Sumanthra went to the nearest holy river, Mandakini, and conducted the after death ceremony of Dasaratha in the river. They all held each other's hands and cried.

Vasishta came at that time with all the mothers. Rama got up immediately and touched the feet of all his mothers and bowed to them. Seetha and Lakshmana too fell at the feet of their mothers and bowed to them. Rama bowed to his respected teacher Vasishta. Rama again told Bharata to go back to Ayodhya and rule the country as per the wish of their father.

Rama said, "I will come back after finishing my period of 14 years in the forest." Jabali muni who accompanied Vasishta tried his best to convince Rama to come back to Ayodhya immediately, but in vain. Bharata then told Rama that he would undergo 14 years' stay in the forest and Rama should return to Ayodhya. Rama was not prepared for that too. Rama finally convinced Bharata to go back to Ayodhya and take over the kingdom.

Bharata then brought a pair of wooden slippers and requested Rama to use it and give it back to him. Bharata bowed to Rama. Bharata said, "The power to rule Ayodhya will be represented by these two wooden slippers. I will stay in the Ayodhya border wearing clothes of bark and eat fruits and roots like you for 14 years and rule the country. If you do not return after 14 years, I will commit suicide by immolating myself."

Rama agreed to this. He advised Bharata and Shatrughna to take care of their mothers with affection and behave with kindness and love to Kaikeyi. Rama returned to the ashram after requesting everybody to return to Ayodhya.

Bharata with the wooden slippers on his head, got in the chariot with Shatrughna. With the Brahmins leading the way, they all left the Mandakini River. Bharata went to Bharadwaja muni's ashram and bowed to the sage. He informed the sage about Rama's decision of not coming back to Ayodhya now. They returned in the same way and reached Ayodhya. Bharata decided to live in the village of Nandigram as an ascetic and rule the country. He accordingly informed Sumanthra and all other ministers. Bharata and Shatrughna thus went straight to Nandigram. Bharata kept the wooden slippers on the throne and started ruling Ayodhya.

In Chitrakoot, Rama felt that the sanyasis were anxious about some matter. Rama asked the ascetics, "What is the problem? I hope that neither my brother, wife or I have done anything to offend you. I hope our conduct has been satisfactory."

They told Rama, "You have not done anything wrong. The younger brother of Ravana, Khara, and his friends are threatening the people here. They appear here in huge fearful shapes. They throw filthy and inauspicious objects in the holy fire and make it unholy. We have therefore decided to leave this place and go to Athri muni's ashram."

Rama was unhappy to remain in his ashram. "The memories of my mothers and Bharata haunts me. Let us also go to Athri muni's ashram." They reached Athri muni's ashram where the aged muni lived with his wife Anasuya. Athri muni extolled about the virtues of his wife. Seetha paid homage to Anasuya. Anasuya spoke to

Seetha lovingly. Anasuya then asked Seetha for a boon; and said she would fulfil that wish. Seetha said, "Your holy mother's presence itself is a great blessing to me. I do not have any such desires."

Anasuya gave Seetha a divine dress, ornaments, cosmetics and cream. Anasuya blessed her saying that these ornament and dresses would keep her young and beautiful forever. She sent Seetha to Rama, decked in the dress and ornaments. Rama was delighted on hearing about the gifts Anasuya had given Seetha. They stayed the night there.

In the morning, they prepared to leave. Rama asked Athri muni the way to Dandaka Forest. Athri muni told them to be very careful since the forest was full of wild animals and cruel rakshasas. Rama, Seetha and Lakshmana then bowed to Athri muni and Anasuya and said goodbye to them.

❑

Chapter 3
Aaranya Kanda

Killing of Viradha and Visiting Sharabhanga Muni

This chapter starts with Ram, Seetha and Lakshmana entering the Dandaka Forest, then reaching Sharabhanga muni's ashram and meeting Shabari.

The Dandaka Forest was a very beautiful place, perfect for a tranquil ashram. A huge monstrous being came to them as soon as they entered the forest. His name was Viradha. Seeing that Seetha was an incarnation of Goddess Lakshmi, he caught hold of Seetha and said, "I will make her my wife. If you do not allow that, I will kill both of you. My father is Java and my mother is Shathahrada. I have obtained a special boon from Brahma that I cannot be killed by any weapon."

Rama was furious on hearing this and showered seven arrows on Viradha. Viradha fell down and dropped Seetha from his hands. Rama cut off his right hand and Lakshmana his left hand. They then fought him with their bare hands and Viradha became unconscious. Rama told Lakshmana to dig a pit and put Viradha in it and cover him with mud. When Lakshmana was digging the pit, Viradha regained consciousness. He then told Rama, "I am not a rakshasa but a gandharva named Thumburu. Kubera cursed me and I became a rakshasa. Kubera told me that I will regain my gandharva form only if I meet Rama and gain his blessings." Rama placed Viradha's body under his feet and put him inside the pit and covered him with stones and mud. Thus Viradha went to heaven. Before leaving, Thumburu advised Rama to go meet the great Sharabhanga muni.

Rama, Lakshmana and Seetha went to Sharabhanga's ashram as per the advice of Thumburu. Indra was in conversation with Sharabhanga muni at that time. Indra immediately disappeared as he wanted to see Rama only after the killing of Ravana. All three bowed to the muni and touched his feet as a sign of respect. Rama asked the muni, "Excuse me, the question may appear to be inappropriate, but what was the purpose of Indra's visit?"

The muni said, "With my yogic powers, I can ascend to heaven. Indra had come here to take me. Just then, we received the message of your arrival. I wanted to see you, O Rama, before my death. So, I waited for you."

Rama asked Sharabhanga muni to suggest a suitable place for them to stay during their stay in the forest. He told Rama to meet Sutheekshna muni. Sharabhanga muni told Rama that the time had come for him to give up his physical body. "I have a desire that it should be in your presence." The muni invoked the sacrificial fire and offered ghee in it and jumped into the fire. His body turned into ashes. Immediately, he came out from the fire with a radiant new body and disappeared into the sky to go to heaven.

A few rishis, knowing Rama was there, came and asked Rama to protect them from the attack of rakshasas. Rama promised to protect them. Rama with Seetha and Lakshmana reached

Sutheekshna muni's ashram along with the rishis. The muni welcomed them and told Rama that Indra had informed him about his visit. Rama asked the muni, "Please suggest a place where we can stay." The muni told them that they were welcome to stay in his ashram. Rama did not accept the offer. But they did agree to stay there that night.

The next day, they resumed their journey after taking leave from the muni. Along the way, Seetha started a conversation about sins. "There are three types of sins: Telling lies, wanting someone else's property and killing innocent people. You are free from the first two sins. But you always carry a bow and arrow with you. Do not kill innocent animals and rakshasas with it."

Rama told Seetha, "I have already given a promise to the rishis that I will protect them from the rakshasas. I will only carry out that duty."

They walked for a long time and reached the shore of a lake. The sound of music was coming out from the water. Dharmabhrita muni, who was with them explained, "This lake was built by Mandakarni muni. He spent years in it, practicing severe austerities. The gods sent five apsaras to disturb his penance. The muni married them and built a house for them. The music we are hearing is coming from their playing musical instruments."

Rama, Lakshmana and Seetha stayed in many ashrams in the Dandaka Forest for a period of fifteen to thirty days and spent about ten years there. At this period of time, they returned to Sutheekshna muni's ashram. One day, Rama informed Sutheekshna muni about his desire to meet Agastya muni. Rama said, "I have come to know that the great sage Agastya is staying nearby. Please tell us where it is. We want to go and meet him and pay him our respects."

Sutheekshna muni showed them the way. They accordingly proceeded to Agastya muni's ashram. They reached the ashram of Agastya muni's brother before dusk. Agastya muni's brother received them. They stayed there and started their journey to

Agastya muni's ashram next day. A disciple of Agastya muni was waiting for Rama and took them to Agastya muni. Rama prostrated in front of the muni, who gifted Rama with a divine bow created by Viswakarma for Lord Vishnu, two quivers given by Indra which never went empty, and a golden sword used by Lord Vishnu to fight his enemies. He told Seetha, "Your fame will always remain in the world due to your devotion to your husband during this difficult period." Rama asked the muni to tell him a suitable place for them to stay during their rest of their stay in the forest.

Travel to Panchavati, and Cutting the Nose and Ears of Shoorpanakha

Agastya muni thought for a while and then told Rama, "There is a very beautiful place called Panchavati near the banks of the River Godavari. It is about seven kms away from here."

On their way to Panchavati they saw a mighty eagle. The eagle told them, "I was a close friend of your father. Kashyapa muni married eight daughters of Daksha Prajapathi. Vinatha, who is of the lineage of Prajapathi gave birth to Aruna, and Thamasi gave birth to Shyeni. I am the son of Aruna and Shyeni and my name is Jatayu. I want to be your obedient servant and serve you. This place is full of wicked rakshasas. When you and Lakshmana leave your dwelling place, I will keep watch over Seetha." Rama greeted his father's friend Jatayu lovingly. In Jatayu's secure presence they reached Panchavati. Rama then asked Lakshmana to build a hut for them to stay. Lakshmana asked Rama to select a suitable place on the banks of the River Godavari. Rama selected a beautiful place on the banks near a lake where white and blue lotus flowers were growing. The shores flocked with birds including ducks, peacocks, doves and their sounds filled the air. They built a very beautiful hut there and had a house warming ceremony. Rama and Lakshmana would go to the river every morning to bathe and offer prayers.

One day a rakshasi came there. She had never seen a being as beautiful as Rama and she fell in love with him. She asked Rama, "Who are you? Why are you wearing the dress of a sanyasi? Why did you come to this forest?"

Rama having good manners, introduced himself as the son of King Dasaratha. He asked her politely about herself. She said, "My name is Shoorpanakha. I am the sister of Ravana, Kumbhakarna, Khara and Dooshana. I stay here and make all creatures shiver due to my wicked actions. I want you to become my husband and make me your wife. You give up your wife. I am a very strong woman. I will kill and eat Seetha and Lakshmana."

Rama told Shoorpanakha, "I am a married man. My younger brother is more suitable for you than me. You go and tell him and accept him as your husband." Shoorpanakha did not understand that Rama was teasing her. She went to Lakshmana and said, "O beautiful young man, you look very courageous and stronger than your brother. You therefore make me your wife. We can happily live and enjoy our life here."

Lakshmana then told her, "O beautiful lady, I am only serving Rama. If I marry you your duty will be to serve Seetha as her servant. Please go back to Rama and ask him again. He is enamoured of your beauty and will marry you."

Shoorpanakha then rushed towards Seetha to kill her. Rama told Lakshmana, "She is a threat to Seetha. Teach her a lesson."

Lakshmana after hearing Rama's instructions, cut off Shoorpanakha's nose and ears. Shoorpanakha crying with unbearable pain ran away. She complained to her brother Khara. Khara got very angry after seeing his injured sister. He asked, "Who did this to you? Was it a deva, asura, gandharva or a muni? How did he get the courage to do that? Whoever it is, I am going to kill him."

Shoorpanakha said, "In Dandakaranya there are two brothers, Rama and Lakshmana. They were the ones to do this to me."

Khara vowed "I will get satisfaction and peace only if I drink Rama's blood."

Then Khara sent fourteen rakshasas to attack Rama and Lakshmana accompanied by Shoorpanakha.

Rama told Lakshmana to keep a watch on Seetha and spoke to the rakshasas. He told them, "I have given a promise to all sanyasis that I will protect them from your attack. We are also living like sanyasis and have adopted their way of life. Why are you harming us? If you have desire to live your life peacefully, please go away."

All the 14 rakshasas came forward, swinging all types of weapons at Rama. Rama broke and destroyed all their lances with the first 14 arrows. He pierced their hearts with the next 14 arrows. They all fell down dead. After seeing this, Shoorpanakha ran back to Khara. Khara after seeing Shoorpanakha's plight decided to go himself to kill Rama and Lakshmana and give their blood to Shoorpanakha to drink. He asked his brother Dooshana to bring his chariot and arms with fourteen thousand rakshasas. At that time, many ill omens were seen. Vultures flew and the sky rained blood.

Seeing the approach of Khara with his army, Rama asked Lakshmana to keep Seetha inside a cave and keep a watch outside and protect her. Lakshmana and Seetha went to the cave. Rama wore his golden amour and grasped his weapons and shouted at the rakshasas to stop. They ran forward to him, but he took on a bigger form. The rakshasas threw their weapons including darts, tridents and hatchets at Rama. Khara sent a thousand arrows at Rama. Rama was easily cutting down most of the weapons coming towards him using his arrows. Rama was injured and bleeding but he did not feel the pain. He used his arrows to break their legs and arms and also shatter their chariots. Angered, the rakshasas, renewed the attack with even more weapons and arrows. Rama alone stood up to all the weapons and killed most of the rakshasas.

Dooshana also arrived unexpectedly with more rakshasas and attacked Rama. Rama used the powerful gandharva missile on them and killed them. Dooshana was left with five thousand rakshasas who fought back. Rama fought courageously and with a strong arrow, cut Dooshana's bow into two pieces and killed the driver of Dooshana's chariot. Dooshana got down from the chariot and came towards Rama with a mace—a type of weapon used in fighting. Rama with two arrows cut Dooshana's hands and with the third arrow he killed Dooshana. All the remaining rakshasas attacked him, but Rama sent five thousand arrows and killed all the rakshasas. The battlefield was drenched with blood and the soil turned red.

Khara, Thrishiras (a person with three heads), and a few rakshasas were left alive. Thrishiras told Khara that he would go alone and kill Rama and Khara agreed with him. He sent many arrows at Rama. Rama got injured on his forehead. This angered Rama and he killed Thrishiras' charioteer and horses. Thrishiras came down from the chariot. Rama then sent an arrow to Thrishiras' chest, and three other arrows to each of his heads and killed him.

Khara came running towards Rama with the remaining rakshasas and started attacking him. He cut Rama's bow into two pieces. Rama through the pain and loss of weapons, calmly picked up the divine bow of Lord Vishnu gifted to him by Agastya muni. He then sent arrows at Khara. Khara's flag was cut down. Meanwhile, Khara's arrows had injured Rama. Rama sent arrows at Khara and injured him; he also killed Khara's charioteer and horses after destroying the chariot. The last arrow hit Khara's chest and he became unconscious. He regained his consciousness, got down from the chariot with the mace in his hand and came in front of Rama. Rama told him that the end of his life has come.

"You are a rakshasa who has committed many sins."

Khara came forward swinging his mace and threw it at Rama. It was thrown with such strength that it destroyed many trees. Rama cut that mace into small pieces with his arrows. Khara then threw an enormous rock at Rama, but he had cut that too into pieces. Rama sent a thousand arrows together to end the war. Even though heavily injured, Khara as a last resort came forward to attack Rama. Rama sent an Agneya (fire) arrow at Khara which pierced his chest and he died. All the devas witnessed the battle and appreciated Rama's valour. He had killed an army of fourteen thousand rakshasas in one and half hours.

Seetha and Lakshmana were happy and relieved to know that Rama was safe. Lakshmana and Seetha came out of the cave. Seetha then warmly and lovingly put her arms around Rama and hugged him. A group of munis accompanied by Agastya came there and told Rama, "The purpose of Indra's visit to Sharabhanga muni was to kill all the rakshasas. That is why you were asked to come and stay here."

Meanwhile a rakshasa named Akampana escaped from the war. He went to Lanka and met Ravana and explained to him the miserable and sad way his two brothers were killed.

Akampana explained to Ravana about the death of his two brothers and fourteen thousand army men caused by a single person. Ravana then asked, "Did this Rama fight with the help of devas? I am going to kill that person who did this. Nobody including Indra, Yama or Lord Vishnu can save him."

Akampana continued, "Rama fought without even taking the help of his brother Lakshmana. His capacity to fight is very great and his knowledge of war is unbelievable. He did all this in one and a half hours. When Rama becomes angry, nobody will be able to face him in war. He has the capability to destroy everything."

Ravana after hearing this, told Akampana that he would go and kill Rama and Lakshmana right then. Akampana then told Ravana, "Do not jump into a decision like this. You have not really understood Rama and his ability to fight. Nobody can kill Rama, even if all devas and asuras join together to fight him. Therefore, it is not possible to defeat Rama by our strength. Rama has a very beautiful wife and her face is as shining as a thousand full moons. We have to abduct Seetha and take her away from there and bring her here. Rama will be miserable. That will be our sweet revenge."

Ravana said, "I will go to Panchavati tomorrow in a chariot and bring Seetha here."

After Akampana left, Ravana went to meet Mareecha. Mareecha was surprised to see Ravana. He asked Ravana, "Why have you come here? I know that unless it is a serious matter, you will not come here."

Ravana said, "You are correct. Lakshmana, Rama's younger brother cut off Shoorpanakha's ears and nose. While trying to take revenge for that, my younger brothers, Khara and Dooshana, who I had thought are invincible, were killed. Rama fought with them and a fourteen thousand rakshasa army and killed them all. You should therefore help me to take away Seetha from Panchavati."

Mareecha said, "The person who advised you to do this is your enemy. It will lead to complete destruction. Rama is Lord Vishnu's incarnation. Nobody has the capacity to face his bow and arrows. Whoever goes to fight with him, will be killed. O rakshasa king, control your anger and please return to Lanka. You live happily and peacefully with your wife there. Please let Rama too live happily with his wife in Panchavati."

Ravana accepted Mareecha's advice and returned to Lanka. Shoorpanakha who had seen the whole war, and the death of her brothers came to Ravana's palace.

Ravana was born with ten heads. Ravana had prayed and meditated on Brahma. Ravana had then cut off each of his head and offered them to Brahma. Happy with his prayer and meditation, Brahma gave him a blessing that no deva or asura could kill him. Ravana had not considered asking for protection from human beings, whom he did not consider as strong enough to be able to defeat him. He became very proud of his power and started troubling all the munis by obstructing their *homas* (offering in the fire). All the munis went and met Lord Vishnu and explained to him about the cruel actions of Ravana and requested him to save them from him. Vishnu told them that it would happen.

Shoorpanakha showed Ravana the injuries she had received from Lakshmana and she started crying, "O brother, you are not seeing all the dangers that are coming to you. You are only interested in enjoying your life. Are your spies not furnishing you with the latest information about the danger you are going to face? Did you not know that your two brothers and fourteen thousand army men were killed by Rama alone? In spite of knowing all this, you are not acting in a responsible way. You are not behaving in a manner that befits a king. If you continue like this, you will lose your kingdom."

Ravana got very angry on hearing this, but he controlled himself. Ravana then asked, "Who is this Rama? Is he extremely strong? Did he cut off your ears and nose? Tell me, I want to know everything."

Shoorpanakha said, "Rama has very beautiful eyes like a lotus, long strong hands and legs, and a very attractive body. Lakshmana is his younger brother who cut off my ears and nose. The name of Rama's wife is Seetha. She is very beautiful like Lakshmi Devi, with wide beautiful eyes, and her face shines like many full moons. Her skin is like molten gold. Seetha will be a suitable wife for you. I had gone there with the idea of taking her away and to give her as a gift to you. If you are courageous you should bring her somehow to Lanka."

Ravana Abducting and Taking Seetha to Lanka

After hearing Shoorpanakha, Ravana decided to make Seetha his own. Ravana again went to meet Mareecha. Mareecha courteously welcomed Ravana. Mareecha asked Ravana the purpose of this second visit. Ravana said, "I do not have any peace after hearing the death of my two brothers and army men. I have decided to abduct Seetha and take her to Lanka. I want your help in this matter. I have already made a plan. You have to take the shape of a golden deer with white spots on the body. You have to run in front of Seetha and encourage her to follow you. She will want to have the deer as a pet and will tell Rama to catch it for her. When Rama goes away from Seetha I will come there and take her like a thief. When Rama becomes sad after losing Seetha, I will be able to defeat him easily."

Mareecha got worried and scared after hearing this. Then he told Ravana, "It is better if you take back your decision. It will lead to doom for Lanka, all the rakshasas and for you too. You do not know the immense strength Rama has. I will tell you about that and then you take a decision. I was very proud of my strength which no other human being had. I was eating and living on the flesh of munis of Dandaka Forest. Viswamitra asked Rama, Dasaratha's son, to give protection to their fire offerings (*homa*). With only one arrow, he threw me to the distant sea. After that, I took the shape of a beast with fiery tongue and very sharp horns to drink the blood of munis. Rama with three arrows, killed my three friends. I ran back from there, fearing for my safety. Rama will not attack the person who is running for his life. That is how I saved myself. The fear of Rama started in me from that day. Whenever I see a tree, I will feel it is Rama. I would request you to go back on your decision. Taking another one's wife like a thief is a big crime and a sin too. You have many wives. Please live happily and proudly in Lanka with them."

Ravana became very angry after hearing these words and told Mareecha, "I have not come here to hear your advice. I have come here to take your help to steal Seetha away and not to hear the advice from a minister. There will not be any change in the decision I have already taken. It is your duty to obey my orders. I want you to take the shape of a golden deer and attract Seetha. Seetha will request Rama to catch and bring the deer. By cunning, you must lead Rama to the interior of the forest. Then you must shout 'O Seetha, O Lakshmana'. Lakshmana will then leave Seetha alone and run to the help of Rama. If you do not agree to do what I say, I will kill you. You have two options, either get killed by me or get killed by Rama."

Mareecha said, "As a minister, it is my duty to give you correct truthful advice, even if it is not liked by you. When death is nearing, nobody listens to good advice. O king, it is better to get killed by Rama than getting killed by you. Let us now do as you desire."

Ravana hugged Mareecha in happiness. They started their journey to Dandak aranya in Ravana's Puskpaka vimana and reached Rama's ashram.

Mareecha took the shape of a golden deer with white spots on the body. The tail of the deer shown like the rainbow, which is the bow of Lord Indra. The deer was very attractive and eye-catching and resplendent. It started running and hopping around Rama's house to attract the attention of Seetha. All the other animals of the forest ran away and escaped from there. After sniffing the golden deer, they had realised that it was a rakshasa in disguise. Seetha gazed at the deer in wonder. Seetha then called out to Rama and Lakshmana to come out immediately. Rama and Lakshmana came out and saw the golden deer. Lakshmana had a doubt. "This must be the rakshasa called Mareecha who has the habit of taking the shape of any animal."

Seetha's brain had dullened due to the attraction of the beautiful deer. She asked Rama to catch the deer and bring it for her as a pet animal. "O Rama, this is such a beautiful animal. It has stolen my heart. We can take it to Ayodhya when it is time to leave."

Rama too was attracted by the beauty of the deer. He was glad to catch the deer for Seetha. Rama told Lakshmana that he would try to catch the deer alive. "If Mareecha turns out to be the deer, I will kill him. All the munis will be very happy about this. You remain here and protect Seetha with your bow and arrows."

Rama ran out to catch the deer, carrying his bow and arrows. The deer had disappeared by that time. Rama entered the forest. The deer ran and disappeared. Then the deer appeared again and led Rama deep into the forest. Rama was tired by then and took rest under a tree. The deer appeared again. By the time Rama got up the deer disappeared. Rama was angry by now and thought that killing the deer was the only option left. He took the Brahmasthra and sent it at the deer. After getting hit by Rama's arrow, Mareecha fell and took the shape of a huge rakshasa. As per the instruction of Ravana, he cried out imitating Rama's voice, "O Lakshmana, O Seetha," and after that he died.

Rama understood the trickery of Mareecha. He was afraid of what Lakshmana and Seetha would think and do. Rama hastened back towards his residence. After hearing Rama crying out, Seetha asked Lakshmana to go and protect Rama. "I feel fear in my heart after hearing my husband cry. He might be being attacked by rakshasas. So go to his help at once."

Since Lakshmana had promised Rama that he would protect Seetha, he kept quiet and did not say anything. Seetha became agitated.

She asked, "Is it your desire that Rama should get into danger? If Rama dies, do you desire to make me your wife? I will not allow that rather I will die."

After hearing this from Seetha, Lakshmana said, "That voice was that of Mareecha. Nobody including the devas can do any harm to Rama. He has incredible skill and prowess. I had promised my brother that I will protect you. I have to obey him."

Seetha was wild with anger after hearing this. She said, "You cruel person. Are you enjoying the bad luck of Rama? Are you planning with Bharata to take over the kingdom?"

After hearing her cruel and piercing sharp words, Lakshmana had a shock. Lakshmana then told Seetha, "O princess of Mithila kingdom, I considered you equal to a devatha. I can't use cruel and bad words and reply to you. O daughter of Janaka king, I am going in search of Rama on your insistence. I am now seeing a lot of bad omens. When we come back, will you even be here?"

The right time for Ravana had arrived. Ravana was dressed as a sanyasi, wearing a saffron-coloured dress with wooden slippers, holding a stick in one hand and a begging bowl in the other hand.

Seetha was crying, thinking about her beloved husband Rama. Ravana came in this disguise and stood in front of the door of Seetha's house. Ravana spoke sweetly to her. He said, "O beautiful lady, why are you staying in this dense forest alone? Are you a divine lady with magical powers? You are more beautiful than Goddess Lakshmi Devi. Are you an apsara or Rati Devi herself? There will not be a more beautiful lady like you on the earth or in heaven. You deserve to be a princess wearing golden ornaments, beautiful dresses and a lot of servants to serve you. Why are you living in this forest, where wild animals and rakshasas roam?"

Even though Ravana praised her in this manner, Seetha kept quiet without insulting him and welcomed him because she did not like to insult a Brahmin. She asked him to sit down, and offered him water and food. Seetha then introduced herself, "I am the daughter of Mithila king, Janaka. I am the darling wife of Rama." She then described all the incidents that led them to come and stay in the forest. She then asked the Brahmin to reveal his identity. "Why are you travelling alone, O Brahmana?"

Ravana then started revealing the details of his identity, "I am the rakshasa king, Ravana. All the devas shiver with fear after hearing my name. O Seetha, you should come with me as my princess. There will be thousands of servants to serve you. You should give up staying in this forest and come with me to Lanka. I live in a beautiful palace in Lanka and we can happily stay there."

Seetha got very angry and said, "My husband Rama remains steady like a rock and patient like the ocean. He is handsome, mighty and brave and is the epitome of all goodness. I will always be loyal to him. Rama is a lion and I am a lioness. Don't think that you can take me away from him." Seetha was afraid and trembled with fear.

Ravana who understood, told her, "I am the half-brother of Kubera. After driving him away from Lanka, I have taken over the possession of his Pushpaka vimana too."

Seetha then said, "How is it that you are behaving in a very despicable manner if you are the brother of Kubera? If you are trying to harm my womanhood, remember that you are a cursed person for your sins."

Ravana lost his patience and took his huge shape with ten heads, twenty hands and big sharp teeth. He lifted Seetha up and entered his plane.

Seetha started crying aloud, saying, "O Rama, Rama, why are you not coming to save me? Punish this cruel rakshasa." Seetha saw Jatayu sitting on a tree. "Jatayu, it will be difficult for you to fight and protect me from this rakshasa. Please, therefore, inform Rama about this. Ravana is taking me away."

After hearing Seetha's words, Jatayu told Ravana, "I am the mighty king of eagle birds. How did you get the courage to touch the wife of another man? Be careful. Anyway, I will not look away and keep quiet when you are taking away Seetha. I am giving you a warning. If you do not give up your foul activity, I will throw you down like a fruit from the tree."

Ravana became angry and wild, and aimed various weapons at Jatayu. Jatayu in turn injured Ravana with his sharp beak and claws. Jatayu was also injured by Ravana's arrows. Jatayu shattered Ravana's bow with his leg and also broke his armour. He wounded Ravana's head with his sharp beak. Sensing that Jatayu was tired, Ravana flew away in the chariot.

Jatayu fearlessly flew up and attacked Ravana. Ravana with his sword cut off Jatayu's two wings and feet. Jatayu fell to the ground.

Seetha then cried and said, "Truth, morality, good human quality and goodness in the family has disappeared." Seetha then saw a few monkeys sitting on treetops. She removed some ornament from her body, tied them in the upper cloth of her sari and threw that down in the hope that the monkeys would see it and will hand them over to Rama.

Ravana then crossed the ocean with Seetha on his Pushpaka vimana and reached Lanka. He took her to the palace. The servants thronged around them. He asked the rakshasi servants to look after her. “Give her whatever she asks for, dresses or ornaments. Do not displease her in any way.”

Ravana then summoned eight rakshasas. “My young brothers and many army men were killed by Rama. Go and find out by spying where Rama and Lakshmana are staying. Give me the news of all Rama’s activities.”

Ravana was foolish in thinking that he would be able to make Seetha his beloved wife. With the uncontrollable desire of making Seetha his wife, he went to Seetha. Seetha was crying like a fearful hunted deer. Ravana told Seetha, “O beautiful lady, you should accept me and come as my princess. I want to make you mine and enjoy all happiness and joy in life. I am begging you to touch your feet. I have never bowed my head in front of a lady.”

Seetha said, “I belong only to Rama. Remember one thing, that you will be killed by Rama.”

Ravana got angry and said, “I am giving you a year’s time to change your mind. If you do not change your mind by that time, you will become the food of the vultures.” Ravana then told the attendants to take Seetha to the Ashoka garden and take a special care of her. “You may threaten her, talk to her nicely, praise her, or tame her like an elephant to make her accept me.” Ashoka garden was a beautiful garden filled with brilliant flowers and fruits. Birds frolicked there. The cruel rakshasis were Seetha’s attendants. Seetha was afraid of the rakshasis and became unconscious.

Brahma at that time called Indra and told him, “Seetha may die due to the ill-treatment by her attendants and her isolation from Rama. Go and feed her the divine sweet dish.”

Indra came to Seetha’s place in the guise of a Brahmin. He with his magical power made all the attendants sleep. Then he went to Seetha and told her, “I am Indra. If you eat this divine sweet dish, you will not get tired for years and will not have any physical problems." Seetha then told Indra to show his real form. Indra then showed her his real form. Seetha was ready to accept and eat the divine sweet dish. Then she offered a part of it to Rama and Lakshmana and prayed they should accept it and then she ate it. After that, Seetha was rid of all the physical pains she had. Indra then immediately disappeared from there.

Meanwhile, Rama after killing Mareecha thought about what had happened and what he needed to do next. He wondered if Seetha was safe. "Mareecha imitated my voice very well. Lakshmana on hearing the cry for help, would have come for my protection. I am sure this was a plan of the rakshasas to harm Seetha."

The howling of jackals appeared to be a bad omen for Rama. He was worried by now. At that time, Lakshmana reached there. Rama caught Lakshmana's left hand and told him, "Why did you come here, leaving Seetha alone without any protection? I feel from the bad omens that Seetha was either murdered or taken away by a thief. If Seetha was murdered, I will commit suicide. I can't live without her. Lakshmana, why did you leave Seetha without any protection?"

Lakshmana tried in vain to explain to Rama. "The moment Seetha heard your voice, she became like a madwoman. She started blaming me very bitterly. The sharp words used by her hurt me very much. She accused me of sending you to your death to make her my own. She also told me that I am doing all this for Bharata and came here to help Bharata. Since I had no other alternative, I left in search of you."

Rama was angry on hearing this and said, "These words are not a justification to leave Seetha alone unprotected. You know that no rakshasa is capable of defeating me and I am invincible. You should not have taken her words to heart."

They finally reached the ashram. The ashram was empty and Seetha was nowhere to be seen. Rama wept due to sadness. He asked the plants and trees whether they had seen Seetha and also asked all the birds and animals around. He then sadly said, "My darling Seetha, why are you hiding from me? Why are you not talking to me?"

He wondered whether the rakshasas had eaten her as food or she was hiding in the forest. They searched for Seetha in the forests and mountains. They were disappointed after they could not find Seetha. They searched in many other places as advised by Lakshmana. Rama was exhausted and was not in a position to walk. He started crying, calling Seetha's name. At that time, a deer came there and looked at Rama's face and stood there. The deer raised his head, looked southward and started shaking his head. Rama understood that Seetha was taken by the sky towards the south from the deer's signals. Lakshmana too understood the message of the deer. In those days, people used to understand the language of the animals and birds.

They started walking towards the south. Rama saw the flowers worn by Seetha scattered on the ground. He saw Seetha's footprints followed by the big footprints of a rakshasa. When they walked further, they saw a broken bow, arrows and a quiver. They also saw Seetha's ornaments scattered around. Moreover, they saw drops of blood on the forest floor. "What if the rakshasa killed her? I will now kill and destroy all the rakshasas. Why did not the devas try to protect my wife who was alone in a forest?"

Lakshmana told the angry Rama, "You are a self-controlled, good-hearted person who likes the well-being of all living beings. Please, therefore, give up your anger. From the scene, there appears to have been only one rakshasa. You must not destroy others because of the mistake of one person."

Rama became calm and cool after hearing Lakshmana's words. They continued to search for Seetha in the forest. When they walked further, they found an injured Jatayu with blood all over his body and he was close to death. Rama thought that Jatayu was a rakshasa, who after swallowing Seetha, took the shape of a bird. He rushed towards the bird with his bow and arrow in hand. Jatayu spoke, "O Rama, I tried to save Seetha from Ravana. Ravana attacked me with his sword and grievously injured me." Rama immediately threw down his bow and arrow and fell on the earth next to Jatayu. He hugged the noble bird and cried, "O Jatayu, where is my Seetha? Why did Ravana abduct her?"

Jatayu then told Rama, "Ravana has taken Seetha to his kingdom in the south. Do not get worried. According to the time in which Seetha was taken away, you will get her back. You will definitely kill the rakshasa king Ravana and bring her back." Suddenly Jatayu's breathing stopped and he died. Rama told Lakshmana, "This noble and honourable bird, the friend of my father, has lost his life because of me. Lakshmana, please bring firewood. So I can prepare the pyre." After the cremation, they bathed in the Godavari river and did the ritual and offerings rites for Jatayu.

They again started walking in the forest in search of Seetha. They walked towards the south-west side of Dandaka Forest. After walking for some time they saw a huge rakshasi, in front of a big cave. She caught Lakshmana's hand and said: "O beautiful man, my name is Ayomukhi. Stay here with me." In anger, Lakshmana cut off the nose and ears of that rakshasi. She cried loudly and fled. After walking for some more distance, they heard a big and horrible sound. They saw a grotesque rakshasa. He had no head, his mouth was on the stomach and he had two very long hands. He had a single eye on his forehead which was on his chest. He caught hold of Rama and Lakshmana and started wringing their body. They became helpless. Lakshmana lost his courage and told Rama, "You can leave me as food for the rakshasa. Try to escape from here." Rama then told Lakshmana not to lose his courage.

The rakshasa then started talking, "My name is Kabandha. I have not taken food for many days. I will therefore eat you both as my food. You will not be able to escape from me."

Lakshmana then told Rama that they could cut off both the hands of the rakshasa and escape. At that time the rakshasa opened his big mouth and came forward towards Rama and Lakshmana to eat them. Rama cut off Kabandha's right hand and Lakshmana his left hand. Kabandha's body was full of blood. Kabandha then asked, "Who are both of you?"

Lakshmana said, "I am Lakshmana and this is my brother Rama. We are from the royal family. Rama's wife, Seetha, was stolen by Ravana and we are searching for her."

Kabandha was very happy after hearing the name of Rama. He said, "I thank you for freeing me from my curse. I will now disclose my story. I once had a splendid physique. I prayed to Brahma and got a blessing of a very long life. I once disturbed a rishi named Sthoolashiras, assuming a horrifying shape. He then cursed me that I would have my horrifying body permanently. I requested him to grant me a boon to escape from this curse. The rishi then said that when Rama would come and cremate my body, I would get my original body. Indra was my enemy. I challenged Indra to a war. Indra with his Vajrayudha, pushed my head and legs inside the body. I asked Indra how I would live for a long time without arms and a mouth. He gave me a mouth on my stomach and two long hands. He said that if Rama and Lakshmana cut off my hands, I would attain my original body. I was waiting for the day when you would come to my place. From that day, I caught and ate all the animals that came in my way. If you cremate my body, I will tell you the name of a person who will help you to find Seetha."

Lakshmana prepared the wood and both Ram and Lakshmana kept Kabandha's body on the wood and set it on fire. Kabandha came out from the centre of the fire in his original beautiful body along with a divine chariot. He sat in the chariot and told Rama, "You are struck with grief due to the separation of Seetha from you. There is a person who is suffering like you. He is the son of the sun god, Surya, named Sugreeva. He will help you to find out Seetha. He has been banned from entrying in his country by his elder brother Vali. He lives in Mountain Rishyamukha with four other monkeys. You must strike up a friendship with him. You must now travel to the shores of Pampa River where the muni named Mathanga has his ashram. Rishyamukha is in front of the Pampa. Sugreeva is staying in Rishyamukha in a cave fearing his elder brother Vali. Sugreeva is very intelligent, courageous, strong and very broad-minded. Make an agreement with him. He knows about all the rakshasas on the earth. His monkeys can go around the earth and find Seetha."

After saying this, Kabandha went to heaven with the permission of Rama. Rama and Lakshmana walked for some more distance and reached the River Pampa and found Mathanga muni's ashram. They went to the ashram, where Shabari welcomed them with folded hands. She gave them water to wash their feet and hands. She also gave them fruits and roots for food and water to drink. Rama enquired about Shabari's well-being. Shabari said, "After seeing you, my mediation has become fruitful. The munis whom I used to take care of went to heaven in a divine chariot. While going, they assured me that when I meet you, I too will be able to go to heaven." Shabari showed all the beautiful gardens on the banks of the River Pampa to Rama and Lakshmana. Later, the divine old lady, made a fire with woods and with the permission of Rama jumped in the fire. Shabari came out from the fire after some time and went to heaven. Thus, Rama and Lakshmana witnessed the divine meditative lady's end.

Rama and Lakshmana then bathed in the River Pampa and started their journey to meet Sugreeva.

❑

Chapter 4
Kishkindha Kanda

This chapter starts from the time Rama and Lakshmana meet Sugreeva and to the time Hanuman gets ready to leap to Lanka.

Meeting Hanuman and Sugreeva

The River Pampa was a very beautiful place in the spring season. But Rama couldn't enjoy the scenery as he was sad thinking about Seetha and told Lakshmana to return to Ayodhya. "I will somehow spend my time here and die." Lakshmana after hearing this told Rama to give up all sadness. "Seetha is not dead. We will take revenge on Ravana, wherever he is, so give up your sorrow." After hearing Lakshmana's words, they started their journey to Mountain Rishyamukha.

Sugreeva had spotted Rama and Lakshmana from a distance. He looked at them attentively. He was afraid, worried and was jumping from tree to tree. He was afraid that Vali may have sent them. Then Hanuman told Sugreeva, "Do not be afraid of Vali. I feel that they are some divine men with weapons in their hands."

Sugreeva sent Hanuman to find out the details about the two persons who are coming towards them. He also told Hanuman to praise them to find out whether they are friends or foes. Hanuman took the guise of a Brahmachari and went and met Rama and Lakshmana. Hanuman told them, "I feel you are very courageous people. Even though you are dressed like ascetics, your physique shows you are warriors. I am Hanuman, the son of Vayu. I have the ability and power to travel anywhere and take any body shape. Sugreeva has sent me to welcome you with all required courtesies."

Rama after hearing this told Lakshmana, "We are searching for Sugreeva and Hanuman is his minister. He talks very eloquently, is intelligent, well behaved and his heart, voice and intelligence are in union. Please explain to Hanuman the incidents that led us to reach here."

Killing of Vali and Crowning Sugreeva as the King

Lakshmana then told Hanuman, "We are very lucky to have met you. We were searching for Sugreeva. We wanted to meet him and come to an arrangement with him. I am Lakshmana, the younger brother of Rama, son of King Dasaratha. Dasaratha had decided to make Rama the king. But due to some reasons he had to leave the kingdom and stay in the forest. The rakshasa king Ravana has abducted his wife Seetha. When we were wandering in the forest in search of Seetha, we met a rakshasa named Kabandha. He got salvation when we killed him. He was the one who told us that Sugreeva would be able to help us in locating Seetha. We are prepared to do anything for your monkey king." Lakshmana's eyes were wet with tears when he finished.

Hanuman consoled Lakshmana and said, "Sugreeva too has lost his wife and country like you. Sugreeva and his aides will help you to find Seetha." Hanuman then grew in size. He carried both Rama and Lakshmana on his shoulders and flew to Mountain Rishyamukha. After reaching there, Hanuman explained to Sugreeva the purpose of their friendly visit. Rama then met Sugreeva. Rama greeted Sugreeva and hugged him. Lakshmana made a fire and in front of the fire, Rama and Sugreeva took an oath of friendship.

Sugreeva after the oath told Rama, "Dear Rama, from today your happiness is also my happiness and your sadness will also be mine. Hope the same will be with you too."

Sugreeva made a seating arrangement for Rama and Lakshmana with leaves and flowers. They all sat down. Sugreeva started speaking, "My brother Vali banished me from my country. He forcibly took my wife too. I am living in fear from that time that Vali may come and attack me."

Rama smiled and said, "Friendship leads to mutual help. I will therefore kill Vali and take back your country and will give back your wife."

Sugreeva then said, "Hanuman has told me how your wife was stolen by Ravana. I therefore solemnly promise you that I will find Seetha, wherever she might be either in the earth or heaven or underground. Rama, I saw a huge rakshasa taking away Seetha. Seetha was loudly crying, calling 'O Rama, Rama'. When she saw us, she threw down some ornaments tied in her shawl, I have kept them safely."

Rama was very anxious to see the ornaments after hearing this news from Sugreeva. Sugreeva brought all the ornaments and gave them to Rama. Rama could easily recognise the ornaments. Rama felt sad and started crying. He then asked Lakshmana whether he could recognise them. Lakshmana said, "I touch her feet and bow to her every day. I can therefore recognise what she wore on the foot, the anklet. I can't recognise the other ornaments."

Rama asked Sugreeva whether he knew anything about Ravana. Sugreeva said, "I have not heard that name, but I will help you to find out about Ravana. Please do not worry or be sad about it."

The words of Sugreeva gave consolation to Rama. They then hugged each other. They again sat on the branch of a sala tree.

Rama then said, "I am your friend and I am prepared to offer you any help. I promise to kill Vali. You have to tell me now how the enmity between you two brothers grew so much."

Sugreeva told them his story. "Since I believe you are my real friend, I will tell you everything. One day a rakshasa named

Maayavi, who appeared to have great magical powers came and challenged my brother to a fight. They were enemies due to some incident. It was late at night and I tried to stop him. But Vali was too angry to listen and ran out of the palace. I ran after him. When the rakshasa saw both of us, he ran away. He then entered a big cave. Vali told me to keep watch and remain outside the cave. They were fighting inside the cave for many days. One day, blood gushed out of the cave and I could hear roars. In the loud roaring and shouting from inside, I could not hear the voice of Vali. It was the voice of the enemy. Since I could not hear the voice of Vali, I assumed that he must have died. I then shut the cave opening with a large rock. I did all the formal ceremonies after the death of my brother, and went back to Kishkindha. I was then crowned as the king by all the ministers. I started ruling the country.

"One day Vali came back. He arrested all my ministers. I did not fight with him due to my respect for my elder brother. I kept the crown as a mark of surrender at his feet. He blamed me and insulted me. He summoned all the important citizens, 'I was fighting inside the cave with the rakshasa. The fight went for some days. I killed the rakshasa and his relatives. The blood appeared outside the cave because of this reason. When I tried to come out, I found the cave was blocked by a rock. For many days, I tried to escape and finally managed to push the rock away and came out of the cave. I came here and saw Sugreeva sitting on my seat with the crown. I understood that he had done it to take over my kingdom.' Vali then took away all my properties and my wife too. I was thrown out of Kishkindha and now living in the mountains."

Rama then consoled Sugreeva and said, "I will take them all back from Vali and give them back to you, including your wife."

Sugreeva then had doubt about Rama's capacity to fight against Vali. He told Rama the story of Dundubhi, a rakshasa. Once, Dundubhi took the shape of a buffalo, and asked the sea to fight with him. The sea said that it had no proficiency in war. The sea told Dundubhi to go and fight with Himavan. When Dundubhi challenged Mount Himavan, Himavan also said he could not fight him. Then Dundubhi asked Himavan to suggest somebody who could fight with him. Thus, Himavan suggested the name of Vali. Dundubhi reached Kishkindha. It kicked its legs and bellowed terrifyingly. Vali caught the buffalo by the horns, lifted it, swirled it around and banged it on the ground. Blood started oozing out of the ears of Dundubhi. The fight between Dundubhi and Vali continued. Vali lifted Dundubhi, banged him on the floor and killed him. He threw him about 10 km away after lifting and swirling him. The dead carcass fell in the ashram of Mathanga muni. Mathanga muni got angry and came to know that it was done by Vali. The muni cursed Vali that if he came within 10 kms of his ashram, he would die. Vali tried his best to pacify the muni but failed in the attempt.

They could see Dundubhi's huge skeleton from where they were standing. The sight of the skeleton made it very clear how huge the rakshasa was when he was alive. Lakshmana understood that Sugreeva had doubts about Rama's strength and ability to fight with Vali. Lakshmana then asked Sugreeva, "What should Rama do to make you believe his ability to fight with Vali?"

Sugreeva said, "Once Vali cut seven palm trees, each one with an arrow. Rama should be able to cut at least one palm tree with an arrow. Dundubhi's huge skeleton should be thrown to a far distance with his leg. If Rama can do these two things, I can believe that Rama is capable of fighting with Vali."

Rama then threw the skeleton with the toe of his right leg to a very far distance. Then Sugreeva said, "When Vali threw it, the buffalo had flesh and blood and was very heavy. Hence it is not possible to say that Rama has more strength than Vali."

Rama took one arrow from the quiver, and sent it at the palm trees. This one arrow cut seven palm trees at a time in one row. The arrow came back to his quiver afterwards. Seeing this, Sugreeva fell at the feet of Rama and bowed. Rama picked up Sugreeva and hugged him.

Rama told Sugreeva, "Let us start the journey to Kishkindha. You can challenge Vali to a fight. Lakshmana and I will hide behind a tree and watch you."

Thus, they went to Kishkindha and Sugreeva challenged Vali to a fight. Vali came out running angrily. Sugreeva and Vali started fighting, hitting and kicking each other. Sugreeva and Vali looked similar. Rama could not make out Vali. He was ready with the bow and arrow, but could not kill Vali. Sugreeva became tired after fighting for some time with Vali and ran away. Sugreeva thought that Rama must have decided not to help him. Vali told Sugreeva, "I am not killing you now. I am letting you go alive."

Sugreeva went to Mathanga muni's ashram and took shelter there. Rama and Lakshmana reached there.

Sugreeva then asked Rama, "Why did you ask me to challenge and fight with Vali? You should have told me that you were not ready to kill my elder brother."

Then Rama told him, "You two look alike, in your voice, body shape and size. I could not recognise or differentiate between you and Vali and hence I did not send the arrow. Next time you fight with him, wear something which will identify you." Rama asked Lakshmana to take a gaja creeper and place it around Sugreeva's neck as a garland.

Sugreeva again left for Kishkindha, accompanied by Rama, Lakshmana and two monkeys named Nala and Neela. They hid behind a tree in front of the palace door. Sugreeva challenged Vali to a fight again. As Vali prepared to confront Sugreeva, his wife Thara advised him, "Please think about why Sugreeva has come again. There is some reason behind this that we do not understand. Our son Angada managed to get some information through his spies. Sugreeva made a deal with Rama and Lakshmana. Rama is equal to Maha Vishnu. Be careful, because in times when things go wrong, the mind always gives wrong advice."

Vali did not heed the advice from his wife. He shouted in anger and ran out to start fighting with Sugreeva again. Vali was much stronger than Sugreeva. Sugreeva was disappointed and gave the signal to Rama. Rama aimed an arrow which hit Vali's chest. Vali had a divine ornament that was handed down from his father. This was given to Vali's father by Indra. He did not die at once due to its divine power. Rama and Lakshmana approached the wounded Vali.

Vali said, "I have heard that you are very spiritual, are just, courageous and very kind to everyone. But what you did now is cruel and goes against all justice and rules of war. I did not expect this from you. Killing me with an arrow by hiding behind a tree is not justifiable. What wrong did I do? I have not harmed you nor insulted you. I have not attacked your country. If you had directly fought with me you would have been defeated and killed."

Rama started speaking, "You do not have morality and principles, that is why you are blaming me like this. Generally, monkeys have no control of their mind. It is not possible for you to have good knowledge on morality. The king has the right and power over all human beings and animals to punish them if and when required. You were a slave and hungry for power which forced you to do sins. You took your brother's wife and made her your wife. I have now given you punishment for that. The kings who do not punish such people are committing sins."

After hearing this, Vali felt ashamed. He told Rama, "What you said is right. I insulted you due to my pride and ignorance. I realise that I have sinned. Please protect my only son, Angada. My death will make him very sad. Please forgive me."

Rama assured him that he would protect Angada. Thara, wife of Vali came running there with all the ministers and her son Angada. The ministers tried to run away. Thara stopped them. Then the ministers advised Thara, "Don't go near Vali. Protect the palace by surrounding the place. Then crown Angada as king."

Thara then said that she was least interested in the kingdom when her husband was dead. Thara went to Vali. She started crying, beating her chest. She hugged her husband and decided to remain there till his last breath. Hanuman requested Thara, "Empress, please stop this. Your sorrow should not allow you to deviate from your duties towards your son and the kingdom."

Thara said, "It is Sugreeva who has to decide about the crowning of Angada. My aim is to consume my life on my husband's pyre."

Then Vali told Sugreeva, "I ask you to forgive me for all my mistakes. You take over the kingdom. Look after Angada well."

Vali took the divine pendant worn by him and gave it to Sugreeva. He told Angada, "You have to obey Sugreeva. Act only after thinking it over well, unlike me. Keep a balance between sadness and happiness."

Vali died after saying these words. Thara was very sad and started crying, holding Vali's dead body. Neela came and took out the arrow from Vali's body. Thara then told Angada to prostrate in front of his father. Angada after prostrating in front of his father, lost his control and started crying. After seeing Thara's sorrow, Sugreeva too felt very sad. He told Rama that the result of the actions had the opposite result. "I do not feel like ruling the kingdom. I feel like committing suicide by jumping in the fire."

Thara also told Rama, "Life without Vali is unbearable. Please kill me too."

Rama consoled Thara with a lot of effort. Then Rama told Sugreeva, "Now you have to behave in a very responsible way. What had to happen has happened. There is no use grieving over what has happened."

Sugreeva became calm after hearing the words of wisdom from Rama. Lakshmana arranged for Vali's cremation. Thara asked for a chariot from Kishkindha. Sugreeva and Angada placed the dead body on the chariot. They went in a procession to the river and cremated Vali with all the rituals and formalities.

Hanuman then requested Rama to go to Kishkindha and conduct the crowning ceremony of Sugreeva. Rama refused and said, "I have taken a vow to stay in the forest and therefore I can't go to the capital. Please crown Sugreeva as the king and declare Angada as the crown prince and the next king."

When Sugreeva reached Kishkindha he got a very warm welcome from its citizens. The crowning ceremony was conducted by Hanuman, Mainda, Dwivida, and Jambavan. Angada was declared as the next king. Sugreeva got his wife Ruma back.

The next four months were the intense rainy season. They could not go out in search of Seetha.

Searching for Seetha

Rama and Lakshmana stayed in a cave in the Mountain Prasavana for four months. Rama was very sad while thinking of Seetha. He cried, wondering whether she was fine and couldn't sleep well. Lakshmana consoled Rama saying that grief would not help him in finding Seetha. Rama hoped that Sugreeva would keep his promise to get some information about Seetha. But there was no word from Sugreeva.

Hanuman met Sugreeva. "You have to honour the deal you had with Rama. He is not asking you about the promise due to the respect and love he has for you. You have got the kingdom because of the grace of Rama. Call the monkey troops here and get them ready to search for Seetha."

Sugreeva agreed. He asked Neela, the commander of the vanara forces, to gather the vanara army. All the monkeys were ordered to assemble at the capital city within fifteen days, if not, they would be punished. The rainy season ended and winter season began. Winter was thought to be a good time to travel and also to battle. Rama wondered if Sugreeva had forgotten his promised after getting back his kingdom.

Rama told Lakshmana, "You should go to Kishkindha and remind him about the promise Sugreeva had made to us. If Sugreeva has forgotten about it, please remind him and tell him that if he ignores it, there will be bad consequences for Kishkindha."

Lakshmana was furious at this and picked up his bow and arrow. He told Rama, "If Sugreeva is not ready to keep his promise, I will kill him." Rama gave a piece of advice to Lakshmana, "In the beginning, start your conversation in a calm way and behave accordingly. He will regain his memory and remember his promise."

Lakshmana reached Kishkindha. It was a big city made inside a cave. In anger, Lakshmana cut many trees on the way. The gate keepers of the palace saw that Lakshmana was in a bad temper and started attacking Lakshmana with trees in their hands. Lakshmana attacked the gate keepers and they ran away to safety. The ministers informed Sugreeva about Lakshmana's arrival and his angry mood. Sugreeva was with Thara at that time.

Sugreeva's ministers asked the monkeys to get ready with weapons for a war. By then, Lakshmana met Angada on the way. He told Angada to tell Sugreeva about his arrival. Angada went and bowed to Sugreeva and informed him about Lakshmana's arrival. Sugreeva was drunk and almost asleep and did not listen to him. The monkeys were afraid of Lakshmana and ran to Sugreeva to inform him. Sugreeva came to his senses at that time.

The ministers advised Sugreeva. "Please go and make the angry Lakshmana calm with your respectful welcome."

Hanuman again reminded Sugreeva, "The rainy season is over. In the process of enjoying your kingdom, you have forgotten your promise of helping Rama to find Seetha. Lakshmana has come to remind you about it."

Angada took Lakshmana to the palace. Lakshmana heard the voices of songs from dancing girls. Lakshmana pulled the string of his bow and there was a resounding noise. Sugreeva after seeing this, told Thara to go and pacify and calm Lakshmana.

Thara went to Lakshmana and looked at his feet and said, "Dear prince, why are you getting angry with Sugreeva?"

Lakshmana answered, "You husband is too busy enjoying his kingdom. He has forgotten the promise he made to help Rama."

Thara said, "The desire to enjoy things beyond what is advisable is a weakness for some people. Sugreeva as a monkey, has it and there is no wonder in it. In spite of all this, Sugreeva has given instructions to the vanara army to come and assemble here. They will be sent to search for Seetha. Please come to the palace and talk directly to Sugreeva."

Lakshmana saw a lot of beautiful female vanaras in the palace. Sugreeva felt embarrassed on seeing Lakshmana. He got up, folded his hands and bowed. All the monkeys followed suit.

Lakshmana told angrily Sugreeva, "You made a hollow promise and cheated your friend. You are cruel and deserve to be hated. You did not reciprocate the help given to you. I am giving you a warning that if you are not prepared to help find Seetha, I will kill you."

Thara after hearing this, told Lakshmana, "Sugreeva is not a cheat nor a weak hearted person. He has not forgotten to help you. He has already given instructions to the monkey troops to come and assemble here. We are waiting for their arrival. We have heard that the rakshasas in Lanka are very strong. After all the monkeys come here, we will start searching for Seetha."

After hearing these words Lakshmana's anger vanished. Sugreeva got up and started talking to Lakshmana, "I will definitely help Rama. Rama is my lord and master. I am always prepared to listen to him and work according to his instructions. Please excuse me for my mistakes."

Lakshmana then told Sugreeva, "I get angry fast. Excuse me for that. Please go and meet Rama immediately. When he understands your sincerity, he will have hope of finding Seetha."

Sugreeva then gave instructions to Hanuman to ask all the monkeys from the mountains ofHimalaya, Mahendragiri, Mandara and Kailash to come to Kishkindha. Within an hour, millions of monkeys started reaching Kishkindha. Lakshmana and Sugreeva went in a chariot to meet Rama. Lakshmana and Sugreeva stood with folded hands in front of Rama. Rama was very happy to see the monkey army. Sugreeva fell at Rama's feet and showed his devotion to Rama. Rama lift Sugreeva up and hugged him. Rama asked Sugreeva to sit down.

He then told Sugreeva, "It is the right time now to start searching for Seetha." Sugreeva said, "We all are waiting anxiously and with devotion to help you."

The sky looked cloudy with dust. Visibility was low there. It was due to the arrival of many monkeys, jumping from tree to tree and some running on the ground. All the army captains came and stood near Sugreeva. They were ready to carry out their duty. Hanuman, his father Kesari, Thara's father Sushena, Ruma's father Thaara, Ashwini twins' sons Mainda and Dwivida and also the king of bears, Jambavan were present. Rama then said, "First we should find out where Ravana's country and palace is. Is Seetha alive or dead? Form a group for this. We will do the rest only after finding Seetha's location."

Sugreeva then asked the team headed by Vinata to go to the east. Angada was sent to the south accompanied by Hanuman, Neela, Jambavan, Mainda, Dwivida and others. Sugreeva then said, "When you go to the extreme south you will find an island which is about 350 kms from the coast. Seetha will most probably be there." Sushena and his team were sent to the west to search. Shatabali and team went to the north. Sugreeva gave instructions about the path, direction and area they had to travel on in all the directions. Sugreeva had the faith that Hanuman would be the right person to find Seetha.

He then told Hanuman, "You are capable, strong and intelligent. Your ability to solve any problem is much better than all the other leaders. I have hope in you that you will find Seetha."

Rama after hearing this, had faith in Hanuman and was sure that he would find Seetha. He removed the ring from his finger and gave it to Hanuman and said, "My name is inscribed on the inside of the ring. My beloved Seetha will be able to easily recognise that. My dear Hanuman, I am sure that you will successfully complete your duty."

Hanuman received the ring with respect, bowed to Rama and started the journey. Rama and Lakshmana stayed in the Prasavana Mountain for one more month while the monkeys were searching for Seetha.

Rama then asked Sugreeva, "How did you get such good knowledge about the world?"

Sugreeva said, "After I was banished from Kishkindha, I travelled around the world. I met Hanuman during this period. Hanuman informed me about the curse incurred on Vali by Mathanga muni."

The monkey groups who were searching for Seetha used to search during the day and take rest during night. Vinata, Shatabali and Sushena came back after one month of extensive search without finding Seetha and then returned to Prasavana. They did not get any clue about Seetha's location. They came and informed Sugreeva accordingly in the presence of Rama.

The last hope of finding Seetha now was with Hanuman. Angada and his group had by that time reached Mountain Vindhya. There was no rain there and the place looked dry. They were not able to find any fruits and leaves for their food. The time period decided by Sugreeva had elapsed by that time. Angada, Tharan, Hanuman and others found a cave covered by creepers and small plants. Seeing the greenery, they thought that water would be available there and entered the cave. It was dark in the cave. They held each other's hand and started walking forward. They saw a light far away. There was a palace there, with lakes, beautiful plants and trees bearing fruit.

There they saw a divine lady who appeared to be a muni. Hanuman went to her with folded hands. Hanuman asked her, "Please tell us whose cave is this? Everything here shines like gold. We have come here after getting tired and without eating or drinking water for days."

The divine lady said, "The name of this cave is Rikshabilam. It was made by rakshasa Maya as the heaven on earth. He prayed to Brahma and got a boon from him. Due to that, he got all the wealth of Shukracharya. Maya created this for Hema, who was from Indra's kingdom. Indra killed Maya. Brahma came to the rescue of Hema and gave her this place to stay in. My name is Swayamprabha, daughter of Merusaaverni, the devatha of the Mountain Meru. I am a friend of Hema. I am looking after and protecting this ashram. You can take as much food and water as you desire. After that tell me, how did you reach this place which is difficult to find?"

Hanuman was happy with the welcome and courtesy Swayamprabha extended to them. He then explained in detail about Rama, his stay in the forest, and Ravana's return to his kingdom after taking Rama's wife Seetha away. Hanuman asked Swayamprabha, "You have rescued all of us from death due to starvation. What can we do for you in return?" Swayamprabha said, "I have only done my duty. I do not expect anything in return."

Then Hanuman said, "Our king, Sugreeva had given us time for one month, to find Seetha. That time is over. We will have to suffer severe punishment. Divine lady, will you be able to help us in any way?"

Swayamprabha said, "It is impossible to get out of this cave. I will help you to get out from here. All those who can see, can't get out from here. I can help you with my meditation power. You all close your eyes."

They closed their eyes and when they opened their eyes they were outside the cave. The place they saw was green, with fruits and flowers on all the trees. They realised with a shock that spring had arrived and winter was over. Their timeframe had elapsed. Angada was afraid of going back to Kishkindha in the fear that he would be punished by Sugreeva. The other monkeys also agreed to this. They thought of going back to Rikshabilam.

Then Hanuman told Angada, "I assume that you have acquired the eight intelligent qualities that the prince should have. They are: A mind to listen carefully and attentively to what others say; ability to understand the meaning of what others say; receptiveness; good memory power; ability to take a decision on what is favourable or unfavourable; to talk and convince others about your views; ability to analyse and understand others' views; and above all very good overall knowledge."

Hanuman continued, "You should be familiar with four types of political tricks. They are: ability to negotiate and come to an agreement; giving gifts or otherwise please the opposite side; sow ideas in the mind and divide and confuse the opponent; and if necessary, how to attack."

Hanuman continued. "All the great men will have fourteen good qualities as shown: Consciousness about the place and time; no weakness; ability to bear; acceptance; expertness; self-defence; maintaining confidentiality; not uttering lies; courage when facing problems; recognising strengths and weaknesses; consistence in thought and actions; faithfulness; helping seekers of shelter; feeling anger about injustice."

After Hanuman praised Angada with these words, he advised him, "Do not act like a fool. If you hide inside this cave, and if Lakshmana comes to know about it he will come here and kill all of us. Let us go back to Kishkindha. Sugreeva will definitely pardon you. You are also the future king, please behave accordingly."

Angada then said, "You are giving too much importance and greatness to Sugreeva. He broke the promise he had made to Rama. Sugreeva was ready to help only after Lakshmana threatened him. I have decided to live here and die."

After saying this, Angada sat on the grass. At that time Sampathi, who is the elder brother of Jatayu came out from a cave and sat on a hilltop and said, "I have not get food for a long time. When each monkey falls down. and dies I can eat them as my food."

Angada after hearing this told Hanuman, "Our very bad luck. The cruel Ravana was the cause for the death of Jatayu. Next was Vali. Who all will face their fate like this?"

Sampathi then heard the news about the death of Jatayu. He asked, "What happened to my younger brother? Please tell me everything." The news about the death of Jatayu made Sampathi very sad. He was happy that the monkeys praised Jatayu for his selfless action. He then told them, "You should do me a favour. My wings were burnt by the heat of the sun. I can't fly now. Please help me to come down from the hilltop."

The monkeys brought Sampathi down. Angada explained to Sampathi how Rama had to leave his kingdom. Sampathi told them his story too, "When Indra was fighting with Vrithasura, Jatayu and I challenged each other to fly to the sun. Jatayu started struggling due to the scorching rays of the sun. To protect him I kept him covered with my wings. Jatayu escaped from the heat of the sun while my wings got burnt and I fell down on Mountain Vindhyachala."

Then Angada said, "If you are the brother of Jatayu, you will be definitely on our side. Can you tell us where the rakshasa king Ravana is staying?"

Sampathi said, "Though I am not in a position to physically help Rama, I can offer information. I had heard a voice crying for help, 'Rama, Rama'. The person then threw ornaments tied in a cloth and I heard the sound of it falling. Ravana is staying in Lanka which is about 100 *yojanas* away from the south most seashore. I am the son of Aruna who is the son of Vinatha. I can therefore see all those things sitting from here. You will be able to locate Seetha in Lanka who is protected by rakshasa. I want help from you all. Please take me near a river so that I can do the last rites with water for my brother."

The monkey troops were happy because they had got the information about Seetha and they gave up the idea of suicide. Jambavan then asked Sampathi, "How did you know that Ravana had taken away Seetha?"

Sampathi said, "My son, Suparshva, brings me food. One day, he was delayed, in bringing the food. I scolded him for that. He told me that he had seen Ravana with Seetha on the way which has caused the delay. After I fell down on the Mountain Vindhya, I was unconscious for six days. When I became conscious, I saw an ashram nearby. It was the ashram of Nishakara muni. I explained to the muni about how my wings were burnt and I become a handicapped, and hence I want to give up my life. The muni told me not to commit suicide and for everything there is a solution. The muni gave me a blessing and promise that whenever the monkeys would come here in search of Seetha, my wings would start growing and come back to their original form." He then flew away, flapping his new wings.

The monkeys started their journey south. The new information they got about Seetha gave them more energy. They reached the seashore. After seeing the big and vast sea they felt sad, disappointed and wondered how they would cross over this vast sea and reach Lanka. Angada told his group not to give up. He asked all of those to come forward who could cross over the sea. There were monkeys who could cross over a distance of 10, 20, 30, 40 and 50 *yojanas*. Mainda claimed to cross over 60, and Dwivida

70. Sushena claimed to reach 80 *yojanas*. Jambavan said, "In my good old days I could have crossed 100 *yojanas*. Due to my old age I can cross only 90 *yojanas*." Angada then said, "I can cross over 100 *yojanas* to one side, but can can't jump back."

After hearing this, Jambavan said, "Angada you have the capacity for that but since you are the leader of the team we have to send someone else so that you can stay back and lead the rest." Angada then requested Jambavan to find out who would be capable of doing this.

Jambavan said, "Hanuman can do that. Listen to his story. Hanuman is the son of vanara princess Anjana and Vayudeva. Vayudeva told Anjana that Hanuman could travel anywhere like the wind. He would have more strength than Garuda, the carrier of the Lord Vishnu. He has the capacity to do any difficult job. The day after his birth he jumped towards the sun thinking that it was a fruit. He jumped about three thousand *yojanas*. He fell down as the sun scorched him. Hanuman jumped again and Indra was envious of Hanuman's capacity. Indra with a Vajrayudha pushed Hanuman down and his left jaw got injured. Vayudeva became angry. Brahma gave Hanuman a blessing that nobody can win over Hanuman in a war. Indra gave him the blessing that he would have death only when he desired so. Hanuman is the only one who is capable of doing this complicated duty. It is time for Hanuman to show his strength, capability and capacity for war."

After hearing about all his wonderful capabilities, Hanuman got energised. He grew in size. Hanuman said, "I can go around the Mountain Meru a thousand times. When I fly in the sky, I can circumambulate Garuda a thousand times." After hearing Hanuman, the monkeys were thrilled. They told him that they would wait there till he came back. "Protecting and saving Seetha and also saving us from Sugreeva is in your hands."

Hanuman said, "Mountain Mahendra has the strength to withstand my weight and the impact of the jumping force."

❑

Chapter 5
Sundara Kanda

This chapter in short starts from Hanuman jumping from the Mountain Mahendragiri to Lanka, meeting Seetha, bringing back the choodamani given by Seetha, meeting Ravana and burning parts of Lanka, returning, meeting Sugreeva and all the monkey troops.

Hanuman Jumping to Lanka

Hanuman reached Mountain Mahendragiri and prepared to jump to Lanka. Before leaving for Lanka, Hanuman said, "I will bring Seetha or will bring the whole Lanka."

Hanuman pressed down the mountain with his feet and jumped. The mountain started shaking due to the impact of Hanuman's weight and the force of his jump. Many trees got uprooted due to the impact. Hanuman flew like the arrow of Rama. He started flying through the clouds. Vayudeva, his father sent cool breezes his way. Sagara, the ocean wanted to give Hanuman a place to rest. He asked the Mainaka Mountain to rise up from the water and gave him a resting place. Hanuman seeing the obstacle in his way, pushed Mainaka aside and travelled beyond the mountain. The mountain said, "I have come to help you, son of Vayudeva. Please rest on me for a while."

Hanuman told the mountain to excuse him. "I have to reach Lanka very fast. I do not want to rest on the way." As a respect for the mountain, he touched the mountain. Some devas and rishis told Nagamatha devi Surasa (the mother of the nagas) that they wanted to assess Hanuman's strength. They wanted to see if Hanuman had the courage to defeat her or he would get disappointed. Surasa took the shape of a rakshasi and came in the way of Hanuman and said, "I have got a boon from Brahma. I have the right to eat all those who are coming on my way. Please enter my mouth."

Hanuman said, "I am going to Lanka to find Seetha and help Rama whose wife was stolen by Ravana. I do not have time now. When I come back, if you want to eat me you can do so."

Surasa then said, "I am bound by my boon. I can let you go only after you enter my mouth," and opened her big mouth.

Hanuman entered her mouth and started growing in size. Surasa opened her mouth wider. Hanuman grew some more. Surasa also opened her mouth wider. Hanuman suddenly became tiny and flew out of her mouth and told, "O daughter of Daksha, you acted as per the boon you received from Brahma. Now let me go."

Surasa took her real shape and told Hanuman, "O great monkey, you are very smart. You can go now. Find Seetha as fast as possible and take her to Rama."

Hanuman continued his journey in the sky. He saw a rakshasi called Simhika flying along his shadow. She was huge. She opened her mouth and came in front of Hanuman to swallow him. Hanuman understood the danger. Hanuman made himself small and entered her mouth. He went down her throat and using his fingernails, tore open her chest to come out. Simhika died and fell down into the sea. Hanuman could see the shore now. Hanuman thought that his huge body might cause danger if rakshasas saw him. He therefore made his body his normal size.

He reached Lanka after travelling 100 *yojanas* but did not feel tired. He saw the most beautiful city of Lanka on top of the Mountain Thrikuda. The city had many water lakes blooming with lotus flowers and surrounded by protective walls. The streets were big and wide. There were many tall buildings with a domed top and rakshasas could be seen walking in groups. Hanuman reached the northern part of the city. He wondered how they could conquer Lanka. Only Sugreeva, Neela and Angada could cross hundred yojanas and reach here. He decided to focus on finding Seetha now. The work of spying had to be done very carefully. It was sunset now. Hanuman made himself small. When it became dark, Hanuman jumped over the protective wall and entered Lanka. He felt a bit scared after seeing the city of Lanka. There were many beautiful multi-storeyed mansions there. Hanuman could see everything in moonlight.

Suddenly, a rakshasi stood in front of him. She asked Hanuman, "How did you come here? Why did a monkey like you come to a rakshasa's city?"

Hanuman in return asked her, "Who are you? Tell me. After that I will tell you about myself."

The rakshasi said, "I am the protector of Lanka city. Since you have come here without permission, I am going to kill you today."

Hanuman said, "I have come here to see the great city of Lanka and admire the beautiful buildings and gardens."

The rakshasi then said, "This place is meant only for those who are born a rakshasa. It is not meant for the vagrant monkeys who are roaming around. If you still want to see the city, you have to defeat me."

Hanuman said, "Let me see the city. Then I will go back."

The rakshasi got angry and said, "That will not happen."

Then she slapped Hanuman with the left arm. Hanuman hit her with the fist, but he did it gently because she was a woman. The rakshasi fell down and started crying. Then she said, "Do not harm me. Brahma had once told me that when a monkey comes and defeat me, that would lead to the destruction and end of the rakshasa race. I accept my defeat. You go and do your duty, and I am giving you the full permission for that."

Finding Seetha

Hanuman searched around Lanka city for Seetha by jumping from the tops of multi-storeyed buildings from one to another. He saw the boundary wall around the palace built by the stones taken from the River Jambu. There were about one lakh rakshasas keeping watch to protect the palace. Hanuman saw many beautiful multi-storied buildings which looked like palaces. He could hear the souund of instrumental music coming from inside those buildings. He could not see Seetha anywhere. Hanuman looked carefully inside the palaces of Ravana's wives and also saw the palaces of Kumbhakarna and Indrajith. Finally, he reached Ravana's palace located on top of the Mountain Thrikuda. The palace seemed to touch the sky. The palace was like heaven. There were sports grounds, an arms and ammunition storage area and he also saw the plane named Pushpaka.

Hanuman thought that the palace of Ravana was equal to the heavenly palace of Brahma. Hanuman first entered a palatial room. There were people lying down after dancing and singing all night. In the centre of these people, was a palatial decorated bed on which Ravana was sleeping. He had only two hands and one head. His other nine heads appeared only when required. His body was riddled with scars, due to the attacks of divine weapons like Indra's Vajrayudha and Lord Vishnu's Sudarshana Chakra. He had a kingly and majestic look. Some distance away, there was a palatial decorated cot on which Mandodari, Ravana's wife was sleeping. Hanuman for a moment suspected her to be Seetha. Then Hanuman realised that Seetha after separation from Rama would not be able to sleep in this way.

Hanuman left the palace and resumed his search for Seetha. He climbed into all the palatial buildings but still could not see Seetha. He even suspected that somebody might have killed her. He became disappointed. Sampathi had told him that Seetha was in Lanka. But he could not find Seetha. Hanuman thought, "If I convey the message of not finding Seetha, Rama and Lakshmana may commit suicide and not live. Bharata and Shatrughna might also follow suit. Then what would be the condition of the three mothers and the wives of all the brothers? Should I go back to Kishkindha disappointed?" Such thoughts made Hanuman miserable. He almost thought of killing Ravana. He was thinking sitting on top of the boundary wall of the city. Then he saw the Ashoka garden in the distance. He decided to go there and have a look.

He jumped from there to the Ashoka garden and climbed on top of a big tree. He started looking around from the top of the tree. He could see a lotus pond; the water stream from the mountain top was flowing down to the lotus pond. It was a very beautiful place with flowers and fruits on all trees. Hanuman thought that this could be where Seetha was staying. He saw a temple in the distance. It was magnificent with a thousand white pillars. He saw a woman wearing an untidy saffron-coloured dress sitting on the ground. She looked weak and emaciated. She appeared to be sad and tired. Despite all that, her face glowed radiantly. Rakshasis were surrounding the woman.

Hanuman could finally see Seetha. Her face looked like the full moon. Hanuman had no doubt that the divine lady was Seetha. She was seated on the ground like a sanyasin. Hanuman was very happy and tears of happiness filled his eyes and started flowing. Hanuman spent that night on the tree.

Ravana woke up to music played by the royal musicians, as was customary for the kings. After his bath, he got dressed and came to see Seetha. Hundreds of beautiful women accompanied him. Hanuman concealed himself behind the leaves to avoid being seen. On seeing Ravana, Seetha covered her face and started crying.

Ravana said, "O beautiful lady, why are you hiding your beautiful face from me? You are a divine lady. You should not sleep on the floor like this. Why are you wearing such dirty clothes, not eating enough food, and looking very sad? If you accept me as my princess, you will get the best things in the three worlds like prosperity, all luxurious things, perfumes and gold ornaments. O beautiful lady, do not waste your young days and come with me."

Seetha first only expressed her displeasure and hatred by keeping a blade of grass between them and told Ravana calmly, "A sinner can't reach a high position in society, and the truth is that you will not be able to make me your own. I am in the righteous path and therefore you should give up the hope of getting my permission. You are not following the righteous path and always do injustice to others, and your kingdom will therefore get ruined. Why can't you listen to the people with good knowledge? If you want to avoid the anger of Rama, send me back to him as soon as possible. That is the only way left for you now. He helps those who come to him and he sympathize with them. He is a great man.

If you do not return me, Rama and Lakshmana will come here and kill you. It will not be possible for you to escape from them, like you escaped from the attack of Indra's Vajrayudha. They are going to punish you shortly."

Ravana was very angry after hearing this. He said, "If a man speaks decently, the woman should also speak decently. Your words are very harsh. I should kill you for that. I am not doing that because of the love I have for you. I had given you one year's time, ten months are over now. Now you have two more months left. If you deny my love, I will use you as my food."

Some rakshasis felt sad on hearing this and felt sympathy for Seetha and tried to console her. Seetha started talking again, "Nobody wishes you good in this country. That is why nobody is persuading you not to do this evil work. You are like a hare in front of the tiger Rama. I will be the cause of your death."

Ravana got very angry after hearing this. He shouted, his eyes will red with anger, "I will kill you today." A rakshasi named Dhanyamalini pacified Ravana and took him back to the palace. After that, the rakshasis surrounded Seetha. Among them Ekajata said, "You give up your ego and accept Ravana as your husband. He really deserves to be your husband. He is the son of Vishrava muni, who is the fourth Prajapathi. If you deny this, your life will be in danger." The rakshasi named Durmukhi also repeated the same words. Seetha calmly replied, "You can eat me but I will not in any way accept Ravana."

A rakshasi named Ajamukhi said, "We can cut her into pieces and eat her flesh, drink liquor and dance." After hearing such devilish comments from the rakshasis, Seetha was terrified and started crying. "O Rama, O Lakshmana. Why is Rama not coming now to save me from Ravana? Will Rama not know where I am? Did he commit suicide due to separation from me? Did anybody kill him by any foul means? I am not even in a position to commit suicide."

An old rakshasi named Trijata, who was sleeping till now got up. She described the dream she had, "Rama and Lakshmana wearing white clothes came flying in the sky. Then I saw Seetha wearing white clothes with Rama and Lakshmana on a white mountain. They got into the Pushpaka vimana and went in the northward direction. I saw evil portends for Ravana, Kumbhakarna and Ravana's children. I saw Vibheeshana on an elephant with his ministers. It means that Rama and Lakshmana will be coming soon to save Seetha." She told all the other rakshasis not to harm Seetha and asked them to ask Seetha for forgiveness.

However, Seetha was still unhappy. She thought of giving up her life. She seized a branch of a tree thinking of hanging herself with her braid. Hanuman decided to reveal himself to Seetha. Seated on the branch of a sinsipa tree, he said the following words:

"There was a king named Dasaratha from Ikshwaku kingdom,

He had four sons and the eldest was Rama,

He is invincible, ever living, and is an Avathara of Vishnu,

According to the promise given to Kaikeyi by Dasaratha, Rama, Lakshmana and Seetha had to leave Ayodhya and live in the forest for fourteen years,

When killing Mareecha, Ravana took away Seetha,

An agreement was reached between Rama and Sugreeva,

And sent Hanuman to the south,

He jumped the ocean and reached here,

I am Hanuman here seeing Devi Seetha,

Rama and Lakshmana will reach here immediately to save and protect Rama's beloved wife."

Seetha looked up after hearing the song with the message and saw a monkey on the tree. She was frightened at first. Then she thought it was a dream. Seetha with disappointment and tiredness became unconscious and fell on the floor. When she became conscious, Hanuman came down from the tree top and with folded hands asked Seetha, "O great lady, who are you? You look like a goddess and I assume you to be Rama's wife."

Seetha then told Hanuman her story. She also told Hanuman about the last warning given by Ravana who had given her only two months to accept him. "If Rama does not come for me in this period, I will commit suicide."

Hanuman was happy that Seetha had started speaking. Hanuman told Seetha, "I am the messenger of Rama and have come here to inform you about him. He is all right."

Seetha happily started talking with Hanuman. Seetha had a suspicion whether Hanuman was Ravana's spy. Hanuman understanding the mental state of Seetha, praised Lord Rama.

Seetha asked, "How did you meet Rama? Describe Rama and Lakshmana to me."

Hanuman described Rama and Lakshmana as handsome brave beings. He said, "I first met them on the Mountain Rishyamukha. When Rama saw the ornament which you had thrown down to the monkeys, tears of happiness started flowing from Rama's eyes. To make an agreement with Sugreeva, Rama killed Vali. To reciprocate the help given by Rama, Sugreeva decided to help Rama to search for you and to find you whereabouts. Lakhs of monkeys were deployed for this purpose. It is my great privilege and luck that I could find you here. My name is Hanuman. I am the son of Vayudeva, born to the wife of great monkey Kesari."

Seetha was very happy on hearing the description of Rama by Hanuman from the feet to the hair and tears rolled down from her eyes due to happiness. Hanuman then gave the ring given by Rama with the inscription of his name to Seetha. Seetha said, "I am very happy as if I had met Rama. I owe you my debt for this till my life ends. How you came here in this faraway place to find and see me indicates the greatness of your mind."

Seetha told Hanuman to say more about Rama.

Hanuman said, “Rama did not know where you are, that is why he did not come here. When I will go back and inform Rama about you, he will come immediately to kill Ravana and save you.”

Seetha reminded Hanuman, “You should inform Rama about the seriousness of the matter. Ravana is going to kill me after two months. Ravana’s younger brother Vibheeshana has told Ravana, many times, to send me back. Vibheeshana’s eldest daughter Anala has told me this. An old honourable minister named Avindhya, told Ravana that his tribe would be totally destroyed by Rama. Ravana did not change his mind despite all these warnings.” Hanuman then told Seetha that he would carry her on the shoulder and fly to Kishkindha.

Seetha then asked Hanuman, “How can a small monkey like you can carry me and fly?”

Hanuman then took his huge shape.

Seetha then said, “You can carry me. But it will be a bad name for Rama. Hence Rama should come here, kill the wicked Ravana and take me. It is essential to keep the name and fame of Rama.”

Hanuman then said, “I now know that you are really the honest and loving Devi of Rama from your conversation and appearance. I will therefore go to meet Rama quickly. You have to give me a token to show Rama the proof of your identity.”

Seetha said, “When we were staying in Chithrakoot, a crow came there and tried to attack me with its beak. I tried to shoo it away but it flew away and came back again. Then it came and wounded me on my chest with its sharp claws.

The wound started bleeding. This blood fell on Rama’s body. Rama took a small blade of *darbha* grass and gave it the power of the Brahmasthra and sent it towards the crow. The crow really was Indra’s son Jayantha. Nobody was able to save Jayantha including Indra. Then the crow came and asked Rama to save and forgive him. Rama who is very kind, pardoned him, but told him that once the Brahmasthra is sent, it can't be taken back. Hence, the crow lost one of its eyes. The crow which was saved from his life, bowed to Rama and went away. Why did not Rama, who could send a Brahmasthra at a crow not come here and save me? It may be my fate or due to my previous birth's actions (karma)."

Hanuman said, "O Seetha, Rama is very much immersed in the sea of sorrow."

Seetha then took out a hair ornament and gave it to Hanuman. Seetha said, "This gift was given to me by my mother during the marriage. Rama will be able to recognise that very easily. When she gifted this to me, both my father and Rama's father was present." She also told Hanuman to talk to Rama and coax him to come and save her immediately.

Hanuman said, "Please give up being sad. Rama and Lakshmana will come here immediately and kill Ravana. Devi, all the monkeys belonging to Sugreeva's army can fly like me and reach Lanka. I will carry Rama and Lakshmana on my shoulders and come here. You should give up all your doubts and do not get disappointed. To complete my work here, I have to measure the strength of the rakshasas. I will therefore set fire to Ashoka garden and destroy a part of it. Ravana, after seeing that will send many rakshasas to capture me. I will destroy all of them and go back to Rama."

Hanuman Entering Ravana's Palace and Burning the Lanka

Hanuman uprooted some trees and dashed them on the ground; some trees he threw far away. He destroyed the ponds. He left a trail of destruction all around. The rakshasis woke up on hearing this noise. They saw Hanuman standing in front of the garden gate. They all got scared after seeing the huge Hanuman. They asked Seetha, "Who is this dangerous creature? What did you speak with him?"

Seetha said, "I do not know this creature. I am also scared after seeing him. He must be a rakshasa. You should know, seeing you are all rakshasis."

Some of the rakshasis went to see Ravana and told him about the huge magical monkey who spoke to Seetha. He had destroyed the Ashoka garden. They also said that Seetha claimed not to know him.

Furious, Ravana, sent eighty thousand rakshasas called kinkaras to catch Hanuman. Hanuman after seeing the rakshasas increased the size of his body and thumped the ground with his huge tail. The noise made by thumping his tail was thunderous and it echoed all around. Hanuman challenged them.

"I am the messenger of Rama." He said, "I can kill not only one Ravana but also thousand Ravanas." He then roared ferociously. The rakshasas surrounded Hanuman and started attacking Hanuman from all sides. Hanuman took a big iron rod and killed almost all the rakshasas. Some of the rakshasas managed to escape and ran to Ravana. Ravana got angry and sent Jambumali, son of Prahastha, to capture Hanuman. Hanuman then set out towards the temple of the deity protecting Lanka. Thousands of sentries were posted at the temple and they started attacking Hanuman. He uprooted one of the pillars of the temple and swung it around. He then set fire to the temple. Jambumali arrived on his chariot and aimed his arrow at Hanuman. Hanuman's face and torso were scratched by the arrows. The bleeding Hanuman seized an enormous rock and threw it at Jambumali. Jambumali destroyed and broke the rock with his arrows. Hanuman then pulled out a big sala tree and threw it at Jambumali. Jambumali destroyed that tree also with his arrows. Jambumali again attacked Hanuman and injured him. Hanuman then picked up the pillar swung it and threw it at Jambumali's chest. Jambumali was killed.

Ravana was wild with anger, his eyes became red and he started trembling. He then sent seven sons of his chief minister, Prahastha, to catch and bring Hanuman to him.

Hanuman was sitting on top of the wall of the entry gate. The seven rakshasas sent by Ravana started attacking Hanuman. Before the arrows of the rakshasas could reach him, Hanuman swung down from the wall and started attacking them with his bare hands and legs. This caused the death of many rakshasas. Many rakshasas fell down after hearing Hanuman's roars. He also killed all the seven sons of the chief minister of Ravana. The surviving rakshasas ran away in fear. Hanuman sat on the arch of the gate again.

Ravana next sent five top army generals, Virupaksha, Yupaksha, Durdhara, Prakhasa and Bhaskarna along with their troops. Ravana told them not to consider Hanuman as an ordinary monkey. "He has unbelievable strength and fighting power. Please go catch him and bring him here."

The rakshasa army chief named Durdhara attacked Hanuman with arrows and it hit Hanuman's forehead. Hanuman grew larger, he jumped up and landed on Durdhara's chariot. Due to its impact, Durdhara's chariot was destroyed and he was killed. The other two army chiefs, Virupaksha and Yupaksha, jumped up to the sky and started striking Hanuman on the chest with their spears. Hanuman immediately came down to the ground, pulled out a big sala tree and hit them with it and they died. The remaining two rakshasa chiefs, Prakhasa and Bhaskarna, started attacking Hanuman with a spear and dart. Hanuman pulled out a mountain including it trees and threw it at them. They were crushed. The remaining rakshasas were easy prey for Hanuman. The place was full of dead bodies. Hanuman again sat on top of the wall.

Ravana after knowing the above information sent his son Akshakumar to catch and bring Hanuman. Akshakumar was a very strong, smart and capable army man. There was a very big war between Akshakumar and Hanuman. Akshakumar injured Hanuman with his arrows. Hanuman then increased his body size. He destroyed Akshakumar's chariot and horses. Akshakumar flew into the sky. Grasping his feet, Hanuman flung him to the earth. In this way, Akshakumar was killed.

Ravana, after hearing this, sent his son Indrajith to catch and bring Hanuman. "O Indrajith, the evil monkey has killed your brother, the army chiefs and the sons of Prahastha. Use your intelligence and capture him. You have many celestial weapons at your disposal."

Indrajith had won a war against the devas and Indra. He had special weapons given to him by Brahma. Indrajith came on a chariot and started showering arrows on Hanuman. Hanuman became huge and attacked Indrajith. Indrajith knew that normal weapons were useless to defeat Hanuman. Indrajith then sent the Brahmasthra at Hanuman. Hanuman became unconscious and fell down. Hanuman had got a blessing from Brahma that the Brahmasthra would not have much effect on him and therefore he could not be bound by it. He then considered this as an opportunity to see Ravana. Hanuman pretended to scream in fear and fell motionless. He wanted to be brought in front of Ravana. Indrajith had doubts about Hanuman now. Once Brahmasthra was used on somebody, it couldn't be used again against that person. The rakshasas dragged and took Hanuman to Ravana. On the way, they discussed with each other how they could use this big animal as food. Ravana told his ministers to question Hanuman.

Hanuman answered the questions as follows, "I am the messenger of King Sugreeva. He has sent his best wishes to you.

He had hoped that your country would be prospering under your able administration." Though Hanuman was enraged with Ravana for abducting Seetha, he controlled himself and observed the surroundings carefully. Ravana was decked in silk clothes and gold ornaments. Though he had ten heads, he was attractive. He appeared to be mighty, courageous and intelligent. "If Ravana had been righteous, instead of indulging in cruel acts, he would have been comparable with Indra or even better," thought Hanuman.

Ravana was angry and mentally disturbed, but had some suspicions after seeing Hanuman. "Is he Nandi who cursed me when I moved Mount Kailash? Is he the asura king Bana who has come as a monkey?"

Ravana's chief minister, Prahastha asked Hanuman to tell him the truth about his intentions of coming here. "If you tell the truth, you will be set free."

Hanuman felt comfortable after hearing this. Hanuman then said, "I am a monkey who has the curiosity to see for myself and enquire about everything. I wanted to see Ravana. When I understood that it was not possible, I set fire to the Ashoka garden with the hope I will be brought to Ravana. Then many people came and attacked me. I just killed all of them. I had no desire to attack the rakshasa army. I had got a blessing from Brahma that I can't be bound by the Brahmasthra. I just pretended that I had been tied, thus Indrajith's Brahmasthra became useless. I will now tell you the real purpose of my coming here. I am a representative of Rama who is the son of King Dasaratha. I was in search of Seetha, Rama's wife for a long time. Now I have seen her. You are not capable of fighting with Rama and Lakshmana. Even Indra can't face Rama. You know what justice is and have knowledge about all books like the Vedas. It would be good for you to return Seetha. You have got the blessing that you would not be killed by devas and asuras. Do not feel proud about it. You can be killed. An ordinary monkey like me can destroy Lanka. Then what about Rama who is the creator and destroyer of everything?"

Ravana's eyes became red due to anger. He shouted, "Kill this monkey now."

Vibheeshana advised Ravana, "Do not kill a messenger. All the knowledge you had acquired from the Veda will automatically get lost in such cases. Please therefore control your anger."

Then Ravana said, "Those who do bad deeds should be killed and there is no sin in such cases. So he should be immediately killed." Vibheeshana said, "The Vedas do not specify any case where a messenger can be killed. You may beat him with sticks or shave his head. Dear brother, do not lose your control due to anger. You should not kill Hanuman but the person Rama, who sent Hanuman here. Send your army to Rama and Lakshmana. They are preparing to take revenge on you."

The God-loving Vibheeshana's calm words made some changes in Ravana's mind. Ravana ordered the guards to set fire to Hanuman's tail and leave him. "He will then feel ashamed when he goes back and everybody sees his burnt tail."

As per Ravana's order, the rakshasas tied old pieces of cloth on Hanuman's tail and poured oil on it and set fire to it. Due to heat of the fire, Hanuman got angry and started beating the rakshasas with his tail. The rakshasas tied it more firmly. Hanuman decided to bear it as he wanted to see the city of Lanka. They went out on the streets, dragging Hanuman along, parading him, announcing he was a spy. Meanwhile, the rakshasis informed Seetha that Hanuman's tail was set on fire.

Seetha then prayed, "If my *vratha* (austerity) and *tapas* and good work, have some power, let Hanuman not feel the heat of the fire."

The fire god shot his flames away from Hanuman, and the wind god sent cold breezes his way. At that time, the intensity of heat on Hanuman's tail disappeared and Hanuman felt cool instead of hot and was very much surprised.

Hanuman thought, "What is happening? Is it due to the desire and prayers of Rama and Seetha?"

Hanuman then thought that it would not be desirable for him to get humiliated by the rakshasas especially as a messenger of Rama. He then reduced the size of his body. The ropes around him, loosened and fell down. Picking up an iron rod, he beat all the rakshasas. He then thought of his next plan. He decided to set fire to the grand palaces of Lanka with his tail before leaving. He first jumped on top of the palace of Prahastha, set fire to that and all other buildings in that row. He spared Vibheeshana's palace due to his respect for Rama. Even Ravana's palace was set on fire. Most of the buildings burnt and fell down to the ground. The wind blew and the fire spread to all the four sides. The rakshasas started running around to protect their lives and properties. There was chaos everywhere. Elephants and horses were also consumed by fire. The people of Lanka shrieked in fear. They wondered if the monkey might be Agnideva himself.

Hanuman went around the town, saw the burning city and felt content. He then decided to go and see Rama. Going to the sea, he dipped his burning tail in the water and put the fire out. Hearing the loud cries of the rakshasas, Hanuman felt bad. "Was it right on my part to burn Lanka? Did anything happen to Seetha? Should I have controlled my anger? If it had led to the death of Seetha, it would have been like killing all my masters. If Seetha dies, Rama, Lakshmana, Bharata, Shatrughna and Sugreeva will end their lives too. But nothing will happen to Seetha due to the blessing of Rama and her utter devotion to the divine married life." Just then, Hanuman got the information that Seetha was safe, from the heavenly birds.

Hanuman went and met Seetha she said, "O Hanuman, you have single-handedly destroyed Lanka. I will wait for Rama to come and save and take me from here."

Hanuman said, "Rama will definitely come here and save you."

Hanuman went to the top of the Mountain Arishta. He increased his body size, pressed his legs on the ground, and jumped up. The impact of his weight and jumping force made the mountain almost level to the ground. He roared due to the happiness of going back.

When he reached the other side of the sea, the monkeys heard his roars and Jambavan gave his opinion, "Hanuman is coming and must have carried out his duty successfully."

The monkeys started jumping from tree to tree due to their happiness. Finally, they all saw Hanuman landing on top of the Mountain Mahendra. He then climbed down. They gave Hanuman roots and fruits for food. Hanuman then greeted the elders like Jambavan and Angada.

Hanuman in a single sentence gave them the happy news. "I saw Seetha." His words made them curious to know more. Everybody hugged Hanuman. Angada then sat in front and told Hanuman to describe what had happened in Lanka in detail.

Hanuman described his journey to Lanka in detail including his encounters with the Mount Mainaka, Simhika and Surasa. He also described the magnificent city of Lanka, the palatial palace of Ravana and his beautiful wives. He told them how he had met Seetha in the Ashoka garden. Lastly, he told them how he had set fire to the whole city of Lanka.

"Seetha is well. She is a courageous lady. She told Ravana that he did not have the quality even to become the servant of Rama. We have to immediately go to Lanka. We have to bring Seetha after attacking and defeating Lanka and Ravana. Angada and I have the capacity and strength to kill all rakshasas. Think how happy Rama will be in such a case. I could have brought Seetha with me, but I did not have the permission for that."

Then Angada said, "Brahma once blessed Aswinis' sons, Mainda and Dwivida that they would always be winners in a war. Since they are with us, it will be easy for us to defeat Ravana. We should therefore leave for Lanka immediately. We should rescue Seetha and take her to Rama."

Jambavan after hearing this told Angada, "Think intelligently. We have been told only to locate Seetha. Rama had taken the vow that he would defeat Ravana and save Seetha in our presence."

Hanuman and Angada agreed with Jambavan's opinion. They all then started for their journey to Kishkindha. On their way, they reached the Madhuvan Forest of Sugreeva. It was like a heavenly place. There were plenty of fruits, roots and honey in Madhuvan. They ate fruits and drank honey in the forest. Then they jumped from trees to trees, laughed and played with each other. Seeing the monkeys plucking leaves and flowers, the watch man of Madhuvan, Dadhimugha, an elderly monkey told all of them not to destroy the forest and go back. But all of them insulted Dadhimugha with rough words. Dadhimugha then tried to protect the forest. Some monkeys bit the old Dadhimugha, scratched him with their nails and treated him badly. Hanuman and Angada encouraged them in their actions. Dadhimugha was also attacked by Angada. Dadhimugha managed to run away to Sugreeva who was seated with Rama and Lakshmana.

Dadhimugha said, "The monkeys who went to the south have come back. They entered Madhuvan and drank all the honey. They destroyed the garden. Angada beat me."

Sugreeva then said, "The monkeys must have got the happy information of finding Seetha. They would have only celebrated that happy occasion. Otherwise, they would not have had the courage to do this. Dadhimugha, it is very happy news for all of us. I have to therefore forget and forgive them for what they did."

Rama, Lakshmana and Sugreeva were thrilled. Sugreeva sent a message through Dadhimugha that Angada should come to see him immediately. Dadhimugha then went to Madhuvan. By that time all the monkeys were in a good mood and were calm.

Dadhimugha told them to forgive him for not permitting them to have their food in Madhuvan.

He told Angada, “Prince, your father’s brother has told you to reach Kishkindha immediately. He is in a happy mood on knowing your arrival.”

Angada then told all the monkeys, “We have to immediately go to Kishkindha. Even though I am a prince, I do not consider myself better than you all. I am depending on all of you. Please therefore give me your opinion.”

The monkeys were very happy after hearing this from Angada. They felt that such humility could be expected only from great individuals and they were lucky. They then decided to go to Kishkindha immediately. They jumped up and ran to Kishkindha. Sugreeva saw them from very far. Sugreeva told Rama about the arrival of Angada.

All the monkeys approached Hanuman with eagerness. Hanuman informed them that Seetha was safe. Rama looked at Hanuman with glowing eyes, love and regards. All showed their respect and regards to Sugreeva, Rama and Lakshmana. The monkeys could not control themselves and started discussing what Hanuman had to tell about Seetha. Finally, they were quiet. Then Rama asked Hanuman to describe more about Ravana’s palace and Seetha. Hanuman came forward.

Hanuman first handed over the *choodamani* given by Seetha to Rama and said, “Seetha has unwavering devotion to you. She is finding it difficult to keep herself alive. She told me how you had used the Brahmasthra on Indra’s son who was in the form of a crow. She asked me why you were not using that asthra against the rakshasas. She also said she would commit suicide due to unbearable insult, if Rama will not reach there within one month.”

Rama kept the *choodamani* on his heart and tears started flowing from his eyes. Hanuman said, “Seetha had said that this *choodamani* was given to her by her mother during her marriage in the presence of the fathers of both Rama and Seetha."

Hanuman said, "I was prepared to carry her and bring her back, but she refused. She was afraid of flying. Moreover, she said that it would be proper only if Rama came and defeated Ravana and rescued her. In this way, Rama would get name and fame. Seetha was also worried as to how Rama, Lakshmana and the monkeys would cross over the sea to Lanka.

I told Seetha, 'The other monkeys are more capable than me. They do not have any difficulty in crossing over the sea. I will carry both Rama and Lakshmana on my shoulders' and thus saying this I consoled her and then I came back. Seeing the bad state of Seetha Devi, we should make all arrangements to attack Lanka immediately."

❑

Chapter 6
Yudha Kanda

This chapter starts from when Hanuman came back after seeing Seetha, and it includes the preparation for war, the construction of bridge Sethu, the war with Ravana, returning to Ayodhya and crowning of Rama as the king.

Rama then praised Hanuman extensively. "You have done a great service to me. Only Garuda could do what you had done. Some people who do not do more than what they could do are called the least of men; some do exactly what were told to them and they are called mediocre; and others do more than what is expected of them and they are superior. You found Seetha and consoled her with sweet words, then went around Lanka, displaying your strength and ability for the war with the rakshasas and created a fear in Ravana. I am not now in a position to give you a suitable reward for that, because I have been sent out of my country and do not own anything to offer you. I have only my love from my heart for you." Rama saying this hugged Hanuman.

Rama then asked Sugreeva, "Now that Seetha has been found, how will we cross over the sea and reach Lanka?" He was worried as he said this.

Sugreeva then told Rama, "Abandon your sorrow. If you give up hope, all will be lost. Being sad will lead to failures. I am now very happy because of the opportunity I have got to challenge Ravana. All the monkeys are capable of fighting the rakshasas. We can construct a bridge to go to Lanka. If we can somehow reach Lanka, we are going to win and there is no doubt about it."

Rama then told Hanuman, "I am prepared to cross the ocean either by drying it or by constructing a bridge. Tell me about the security details in Lanka."

Hanuman started explaining, "I shall now tell you how the city was fortified. There are many natural fortifications for the city of Lanka. It is surrounded by rivers and forests, built on top of a mountain. There are protective walls all around the city with four massive gates. From gates, catapults can be launched at the enemy. There are moats filled with crocodiles around the boundary walls. I managed to destroy part of the boundary walls. O Rama, Mainda, Dwivida, Jambavan, Neela and I can cross the ocean and rescue Seetha. There is no need for you to come with the monkey troops."

Rama then said, "I have already taken a vow to go myself to Lanka, to destroy Ravana and save Seetha." Then he told Sugreeva, "This is an auspicious time to start preparation for the war. I feel confident that there will be success from our side. Let us therefore call the army of monkeys and start marching towards Lanka immediately."

Sugreeva and Lakshmana too agreed with Rama's suggestion. Immediately, thousands of monkeys started coming from the caves and trees. Rama told Neela to lead the way. "Keep the weak away, because we are setting out on a gruelling journey. Keep an eye on the enemies and see that no one attacks us." Rama and Lakshmana were in the centre of the monkey army. Rama was sitting on Hanuman's shoulder and Lakshmana on Angada's shoulder. The monkey army roared like lions while jumping up and down to show their courage and readiness for the war. They were roaring enthusiastically, thumping their tails on the floor, pulling and pushing each other with enthusiasm. They marched ahead by going up the hills and coming down, throwing trees and rocks.

Lakshmana remarked, "Nature has blessed us with warm sunlight, good breeze and all the wild animals are calm. This therefore is a good omen and indication of good hope."

They walked day and night. The monkeys ate roots, fruits and drank honey for their food. They drank water from the ponds. Soon, they reached the Mountain Mahendragiri. Rama went on top of the mountain and looked over the sea. Afterwards, they marched towards the sea.

Rama then told Sugreeva, "I have to think about how to cross this sea." He instructed the monkeys to make tents for them. The monkeys engaged in the construction of the tents saw the huge sea for the first time. The gigantic waves crashed on the shore, fishes rolled in the water and they saw many other creatures living in the sea. They were seeing the sea for the first time at such a close distance. The fear of how to cross over this sea to reach Lanka disturbed their mind.

Rama could not stop thinking about Seetha and told Lakshmana, "The concept that passing of time will erase the sadness is not correct. I can't stop thinking about Seetha. My mind is burning with the thought of killing Ravana and saving Seetha."

Ravana at that time was having a discussion with all his ministers and advisers. He felt badly shaken by the strength and attacking power of Hanuman. He said, "We had the notion that nobody could come and attack Lanka. But that monkey could do that. He even destroyed my palace. He killed many rakshasas of our army. I now expect intelligent advice from you all including my gurus. Please give your advice and suggestions. Rama will reach here shortly and attack Lanka. There will be many monkeys with them. They are capable of crossing over the sea and reaching here."

All the rakshasa were unaware of the strength of Rama and used to always praise Ravana as a habit. They suggested, "O dear king, please do not be afraid. You defeated Kubera and made Lanka your own. You defeated Mayasura and made his daughter Mandodari your wife. You are capable of fighting and defeating Rama, Lakshmana and the monkey army. Did not your son Indrajith defeated all the devas and made Indra a prisoner in Lanka? Indrajith can kill Rama, Lakshmana and all monkeys before they can cross the sea."

Ravana's army chief Prahastha said, "We have won against all devas and gandharvas. Why then are we afraid of a man, Rama? Hanuman could do all those courageous activities only because of our carelessness. I shall protect you from that monkey."

The next opinion was from Durmukha. "I can kill all the monkeys. I will take revenge on the monkeys."

The next opinion was from Vajradamshtra. "Do not be afraid of monkeys. I will crush Rama and Lakshmana."

The next turn was of Nikumbha, Kumbhakarna's son, "I can deal with Rama, Lakshmana and the monkeys alone and finish them."

Many rakshasas, thus proclaimed themselves as very capable. They all took their arms, started waving them and were ready for the war.

When everybody was calm, Vibheeshana said, "Dear brother, you can start the war and killing only when you fail at reconciliation, or when you are not in a position to tolerate the opposite side. If we have to win the war, the opposite side should be cruel, inattentive, tired from a previous war or should be a cursed party. The opposite side has Rama who is very strong, have good qualities and also is waiting to take revenge on you. The stealing of Seetha is a big curse on Lanka and it will lead to the destruction of Lanka. Please therefore give back Seetha before Rama comes and destroys Lanka. This is the only way that can be good for you. Your ministers are afraid of you and praising you only to please you without telling the truth."

Ravana in Anger, Walked Away

Ravana instructed Prahastha to keep the army ready for protecting Lanka. Ravana then lied to his ministers to make them feel confident. "Seetha has promised that she would be mine after one year. In the meantime, I knew the information of the coming of Rama and Lakshmana with the army to Lanka. The fact is that two men and many monkeys will not be in a position to do anything against me. But that monkey Hanuman could cause a lot of destruction and loss to us. I have called all of you to discuss these matters with you. I want to kill Rama and make Seetha my own. You have to advise me the ways and means for achieving this."

Vibheeshana said, "Dear brother, Seetha is like a venomous snake, wound around your neck. Rama has defeated everyone he met. Rama is equal to Maha Vishnu. You should not listen to what Prahastha said. I am telling all this for your good future. That is why, I am requesting you to give Seetha back."

Indrajith got angry when he heard his father's brother, Vibheeshana, and he said emotionally to Vibheeshana, "You are a coward, without courage or manliness. The advice from such a person is not required. I have defeated Indra in the war and therefore can easily kill Rama and Lakshmana."

Vibheeshana then told Indrajith, "You are just a boy. You have no capacity to recognise between right and wrong. You are dull minded, uncivilised, with less knowledge, cruel and you are like an enemy leading your father to a dangerous situation. I repeat once again that we should give Seetha back and save our rakshasa families. We can then live in peace."

After hearing Vibheeshana's words, Ravana lost his patience and angrily abused Vibheeshana, "You are my enemy pretending to be a friend. I was living with a poisonous snake like you till now. You are a brother who will not help when the help is needed."

Vibheeshana said, "I will only follow the spiritual and truthful path. I will not support or help you in this case. Your life is going to come to an end. That's why you are not willing to accept my good advice. I will not stay here anymore. I am leaving Lanka."

Vibheeshana Meeting Rama

Vibheeshana along with some of his trustworthy people left to Rama's camp. Sugreeva was suspicious about Vibheeshana and told Hanuman, "He could be a spy for the rakshasas." The monkeys were ready to attack him with rocks and trees.

Vibheeshana then revealed to Sugreeva, "I am the younger brother of Ravana. I have advised Ravana many times to give Seetha back. He did not listen to me so I left him and came to you. I have come here to prostrate before Rama and ask for protection. Please inform Rama about this."

Sugreeva then went to Rama and said, "An rakshasa named Vibheeshana, Ravana's brother, has come here. He has given up Ravana and his family. I do not feel that he is trustworthy. He could be their spy. Rakshasas are cunning and deceitful. He should be killed."

Rama then asked the other monkeys their opinion. The monkeys said, "You know everything. You are asking this because of the respect you have for us. You take the decision and we will accept it."

Angada had an idea. "We must not trust him so easily. We have to carefully keep a watch on him. If we feel he is dangerous, we can kill him."

Shabharada and Jambavan too were of the opinion that he could be a spy. Intelligent and good speaker Hanuman said, "We should not doubt Vibheeshana. He has come here for protection from Rama and he can be trusted. He has come here travelling a long distance and has suffered a lot. Ravana is a symbol of evil and Rama is a symbol of *dharma* and Vibheeshana has understood this. We can understand that from his calm behaviour, good way of speaking and we should accept him as a helping hand."

Sugreeva spoke, "Vibheeshana has betrayed his own brother. What if he does the same to you?"

Rama decided to welcome Vibheeshana and told Sugreeva, "We should accept him as a guest. We have to accept those who come to us for protection, as it is our duty." After hearing all this from Rama, Sugreeva felt compassion and told Rama, "Your words and actions are very apt for your high position. I now feel that Vibheeshana can be trusted."

Vibheeshana prostrated in front of Rama and said, "I am now offering with prayers, my selfless service to you. My life is now in your hands. Please protect and bless me."

Rama looked very carefully at Vibheeshana and asked him to describe the strength and weakness of the enemy. Vibheeshana said, "With the blessing of Brahma, Ravana can't be killed by devas, gandharvas, asuras or nagas. Humans can kill Ravana. Ravana's younger brother Kumbhakarna is a huge and strong person like a mountain. He is strong like Indra. The army chief Prahastha has defeated yaksha leader Bhadra in a war in the Himalayas. Ravana's son Indrajith is equal to Ravana in war. He has a blessing from Agnideva that he can turn invisible. In addition to that, Ravana has many army chiefs. Mahaparshwa, Akampana and Mahodara can take any form or shape according to their will."

After hearing all this, Rama told Vibheeshana, "I have understood the strength of Ravana. Despite all this, I will kill Ravana and I promise you that I will make you the king of Lanka."

Vibheeshana too promised Rama to help him to capture Lanka. Rama had faith in Vibheeshana and hugged him. Rama instructed Lakshmana to bring the sea water. They conducted the crowning ceremony of Vibheeshana. The monkeys were happy about the love and affection Rama showered on Vibheeshana and they all danced with happiness.

Then Sugreeva and Hanuman asked Vibheeshana, "We have no difficulty in facing Ravana and rakshasas, but how will the others cross over the sea and reach Lanka? Can you tell us some way for this?"

Vibheeshana said, "If Rama prays to Sagaradeva there will be some solution." Sugreeva informed Rama and Lakshmana about the advice given by Vibheeshana. Rama, Lakshmana and Sugreeva liked this suggestion. Rama went to the seashore and spreading the sacred grass called *darbha* on the ground he sat down saluting the ocean.

At that time Shardoola, the spy whom Ravana had sent to get the information about the monkey army of Rama came and informed him about that. Ravana then sent another spy Shuka to Sugreeva. He took the shape of a bird and came to Sugreeva and told him, "I am the messenger of Ravana. Ravana has not done any harm to you. Why then are you coming to attack Lanka? What connection do you have with the abduction of Seetha? It will therefore be good for you to go back to Kishkindha and lead a peaceful life."

When this conversation was going on, the monkeys jumped up and caught hold of Shuka. They threw him on the ground, pushed him around, and also cut off his two wings. Shuka cried and told

Rama, "A good compassionate person like you will not harm a messenger." Rama asked the monkeys to free Shuka. Shuka asked Sugreeva, "What message should I convey to Ravana?"

Sugreeva told Shuka, "Your master is a very bad king of your clan. He has forcibly stolen the wife of another person and is a cruel rakshasa. When Rama and the monkeys will come there, Rama will definitely kill Ravana and all the people of his clan."

Angada then said, " This bird is not a messenger, but a spy. He has come here to know our strength. We will lock him up."

After hearing this, the monkeys caught hold of Shuka and tied him with a rope. Shuka complained to Rama. Rama agreed to release him after reaching Lanka.

Construction of Sethu Bridge

Rama then prayed and meditated to Sagaradeva. There was no response even after three days. Rama became angry. "Why is Sagaradeva not coming in front of me?" He asked Lakshmana to bring his bow and arrow. "I will shower arrows at the ocean. I will make this ocean dry. You all can then easily walk and go to Lanka." Rama wielded the bow and strung it. It created a thunderous sound and the earth started to shake. Rama started showering arrows on the ocean. Thousands of waves rose up. All the creatures in the ocean were afraid.

Lakshmana said, "O Rama, control your anger. Do not destroy the ocean. Look for an alternative."

Rama then prepared to release the Brahmasthra and said, "I will dry the ocean and allow the monkeys to cross over. Sagaradeva, I know that you are not ready to help me."

The earth and sky started shivering. There was lightning in the sky. Waves rose as high as mountains in the sea. The creatures in the sea were terrified. Immediately Samudraraj (Sagaradeva) rose up from the sea along with snakes with flaming jaws and stood with folded hands in front of Rama. Sagaradeva said, "O Raghu clan born king! The earth, air, sky, water and fire will not give up their basic character. It is therefore difficult to cross over this wide sea. I can do one help for you. If you make a bridge, I will keep it floating. You and the monkeys can go along the bridge to Lanka, fight the war, win the war and bring back your loving wife."

Then Rama asked Sagara, "What will I do with the Brahmasthra which I have kept ready to send? Once the arrow is kept on the string it can't be taken back."

Sagara suggested one way. "In the north there is aplace called Drumakulyam, inhabited by many sinners. Send the arrow to that place." That place afterwards got the name Marukantharam. Rama blessed that place. It became abundant with fruits, honey, and different types of medicinal plants. Those who stay there do not fall sick. Then Sagaradeva pointed at Nala, a distinguished monkey, and said, "He is the son of Viswakarma. Due to the blessing of his father he is a good and smart architect. This *bhakth* of yours is capable of supervising the construction of the bridge which will also be very strong." After telling this, Sagaradeva disappeared.

Nala came and stood in front of Rama and said, "I have the ability to build a bridge. Viswakarma had given a blessing to my mother that she would have a son equal to Viswakarma. Let all monkeys go and get all necessary things and bring them to the seashore."

Under the supervision of Rama, all the monkeys went to the forest and brought many trees and pieces of rock to the seashore. The top portion of the bridge was made of tree logs. Vibheeshana and his men stood guard to protect them from any external attack. The bridge was approximately 350 metres (100 *yojana*) long and 35 metres (10 *yojana*) wide. The first day, they finished 51 metres (14 *yojana*); the second day they completed 70 metres (20 *yojana)* construction of the bridge. The third day they completed 74 metres, (21 *yojana*); the fourth day 77 metres, (22 *yojana*) and the fifth day they completed the construction. Rishis and devas came to see this wonderful work.

Sugreeva requested Rama to travel on Hanuman's shoulder and Lakshmana on Angada's shoulder. All the monkeys travelled along the bridge and reached the Mountain Suvela in Lanka. The monkeys were happy and excited. The monkeys constructed army tents there. At that time the devas and rishis consecrated Rama with the holy water.

Rama told Lakshmana, "The army should always be alert. There is a bad omen and my mind feels that there will be many deaths. We should therefore get ready immediately for the war." Thus, the army started the march. When Rama saw the Mountain Thrikuda, his mind was on Seetha. Rama made a special army formation in the human form. Rama and Lakshmana stood in front. All monkeys were ready for the war with rocks and trees in their hands. Rama then asked Sugreeva to free Shuka. Shuka wished Rama success and went away.

Shuka went to meet Ravana and explained everything that had happened. Ravana smiled after seeing his cut wings and asked, "Who did this?"

Shuka said, "When I was communicating your message to Sugreeva, many monkeys came and caught me, beat me and cut my wings. I was saved by the good and kind mind of Rama. O king, the monkey army and Rama and Lakshmana have arrived here. Please give back Seetha."

Ravana got angry after hearing this and told Shuka, "I will never ever give back Seetha. I will kill Rama, Lakshmana and all the monkeys. It is a wonder how the monkeys could make a bridge over the sea. You along with Sarana go to Rama's camp secretly taking the form of monkeys and find out the strength of their army and come back."

Shuka and Sarana immediately reached there but could not assess the strength of the monkey army that were distributed in the seashore, mountain and forest. They were spotted by Vibheeshana who could recognise them. They were put behind bars and Vibheeshana informed Rama.

Shuka and Sarana admitted their mistakes and stood in front of Rama with folded hands and said, "We did not want to come here. We were sent here by Ravana to ascertain the strength of the army."

Rama smiled and asked, "Could you achieve your objective? Then you can go back to Ravana. The decency by which we received you should be reciprocated by communicating these messages to Ravana. We with the monkey army will come and destroy Lanka and kill all the rakshasas."

They thanked Rama and with humility wished him success.

Shuka and Sarana immediately went to Ravana and told him, "Even though Vibheeshana put us behind bars, the kind-hearted Rama released us. We could neither assess nor find out the strength of the vast monkey army. Rama, Lakshmana, Sugreeva and Vibheeshana can easily destroy and kill all of us without the help of the army. Rama can himself destroy Lanka and kill all the rakshasas and he has the full confidence for that. We suggest that you give back Seetha and keep friendship with Rama."

Ravana after hearing this, shouted at them, "It is impossible to give Seetha back. If all the devas and asuras come and attack me, then also I will not do that. It is foolish to be afraid of the monkeys. I am not afraid of anybody."

Ravana then went on top of the palace with his spies and stood there to study and assess the monkey army. Ravana asked Sarana to show him all the army captains. "Angada, the monkey prince, is the one resembling the peak of a mountain. Nala is the one who built the bridge. Dhumra is the army chief of the bears. Gavaksha is the leader of the monkey troops. That is Hanuman who set fire to our city. There are many more brave and mighty monkeys. The strength of the monkey army is not countable and may be in crores." Ravana after seeing the army captains, monkey army and Rama and Lakshmana, became mentally disturbed and angry.

He insulted Shuka and Sarana who were standing in front of him, bowing their heads. "You are my ministers but you are praising our enemy. I am leaving you because of the good service you had rendered to me."

Shuka and Sarana, bowing their head and wishing Ravana best of luck in the war walked away. Ravana again asked Mahodara to bring more spies. Shardoola and his group took the form of monkeys and went to spy on the monkeys. Vibheeshana identify them easily and locked them up. The monkeys started beating the spies. Rama again released the spies.

They went back to Ravana and told him, "It is difficult to spy on them. We were identified by Vibheeshana, put behind bars and the monkeys beat us badly. Rama who is infinitely kind, let us go free and we were saved. Rama is capable of destroying the rakshasa tribe, and also the whole world with his strength. You have to prevent the monkey army from entering our border. The are camped on the Mountain Suvela now."

Ravana heard Shardoola and said, "I will not give back Seetha, whatever happens."

He then called the magician, Vidwudjihwan and told him, "I am now going to see Seetha. You should, with your magical powers, make Rama's head, bow and arrows. You should then hide there. When I call you, come with all the magical items in front of me."

Ravana then reached Ashoka garden and told Seetha, "My army has killed Rama. Now you have no alternative. When Rama's army reached Lanka, they were very tired and were sleeping. My rakshasa army then killed Rama, Lakshmana, Hanuman and many army captains. We killed most of the monkeys too. I have brought the head of Rama, his bow and arrows." Ravana asked a rakshasi to call Vidwudjihwan. Vidwudjihwan reached there and Ravana asked him to keep Rama's head, bow and arrow in front of Seetha. Ravana then told Seetha, "See the lifeless head of Rama. You have to now accept what I say. There is no alternative for you."

Seetha started weeping after seeing this and said, "O Kaikeyi, this is the result of all your cruel plans. Your desire is fulfilled now and you can enjoy the kingdom." Seetha started shivering after crying, then she became unconscious and fell down on the ground. Seetha, after regaining consciousness, said, "O Rama, I have become a widow after your death. My life itself has ended here. Living after the death of the husband is the biggest disaster in life. Did you go to the other world without taking me?" She then told Ravana, "Take me to the place where Rama's body is lying. Then you can kill me too."

A messenger came there at that time and told Ravana that Prahastha had called for a meeting of all ministers and he should reach there immediately. Ravana immediately went away from the Ashoka garden. Immediately, the magical head, bow and arrow disappeared from there.

Ravana went to the meeting. He gave instructions to the army chiefs to get ready and prepare for the war. Ravana sent a rakshasi named Sarama to console Seetha. Sarama went to Ashoka garden and told Seetha, "I was hiding behind the bushes here and could hear and also see what happened here. I can give you the assurance that Rama is not dead. The head you had seen was made of magical power and was not real. The truth is that Rama, Lakshmana and his huge army has reached Lanka. They are ready to attack Ravana now. Ravana knows that he can't defeat Rama, Lakshmana and his army. I can hear the sound of the rakshasa army getting ready and preparing for war. There will be a war immediately. Rama will definitely kill Ravana. If you have any message to be conveyed to Rama, please tell me, I can convey it to him."

Seetha was extremely happy after hearing the truth from Sarama. She asked Sarama to find out what Ravana was planning. Sarama heard what Ravana was discussing with his ministers. All the old ministers suggested that Seetha should be given back to Rama. They also explained to Ravana, Rama's courage and war expertise. At that time, they could all hear the sound of Rama's army marching forward. Ravana's grandfather Malyavan also told Ravana to give back Seetha. He told Ravana that an intelligent king would not fight with a very strong enemy. He continued, "You have incurred the sins of many munis by attacking them and their meditation power will be always against you. You have no protection from death from humans and monkeys according to Brahma's boon. O my grandson, take a suitable decision after assessing the seriousness of the situation and its danger. I am also seeing many bad omens. Ravana, Rama is an avathar of Lord Vishnu born as a human. It would be therefore good for you to surrender before Rama. That is the only way out to get out of this complicated situation."

Sarama came back and told Seetha all this. "Despite all the good advice, there was no change in Ravana. Ravana said, 'All those who support the enemy are rogues. Nobody knows how strong I am. All are jealous of me. They have either been prompted by the enemy or afraid of the enemy. Rama will be killed by me.' Malyavan after hearing these words, wished Ravana well and walked away," Sarama said.

Ravana started the preparations for the protection of Lanka. He deputed Prahastha to keep watch on the eastern gate, and Mahaparshwa and Mahodara, on the southern gate. Virupaksha was deputed to protect the city. Indrajith was to guard the western gate.

War between Rama and Ravana

Rama and the monkey army discussed tactics on how to attack Lanka. Vibheeshana arrived with good news. Vibheeshana with Anala, Sampathi, Panasa and Pramathi took the form of birds and went to see Ravana's army. He told Rama, "Even though the rakshasa army is strong, our monkey army comprised of four divisions can easily defeat Ravana."

Rama gave instructions to start the army manoeuvres. "The group led by Neela should face Prahastha's army at the northern gate. Angada will face and attack Mahaparshwa and Mahodara at the southern gate. Hanuman will go to the western gate. I along with Lakshmana will face Ravana at the northern gate with the army. Vibheeshana, Sugreeva and Jambavan will remain in the middle. Their duty is to solve any problem for any group. Seven among us should be in the human form. Lakshmana, me, Vibheeshana and four ministers will be in human form to start the war. Monkeys should not take the human form as this will help us to differentiate them from the rakshasas."

Rama, Lakshmana, others and monkey army reached the top of the Mountain Suvela when it was sunset. They decided to spend the night there. They scanned Lanka from the mountain top. They could see the preparations of the rakshasa army for the war. They saw in the morning light, the beautiful heaven like city. There were beautiful gardens, divine trees, and birdsong from various birds. Rama saw all the wonderful things and felt happy. The vast and beautiful Lanka was located on top of the Mountain Thrikuda. Ravana's palace was surrounded by huge boundary walls and gates. Rama saw Ravana with his attendants on top of the palace. The monkeys started jumping from tree to tree in the flower gardens. Sugreeva asked them to remain there.

Sugreeva also saw Ravana then. Sugreeva impulsively leapt from the mountain and sprang in front of Ravana. Ravana looked at him with contempt.

Sugreeva told Ravana, "O rakshasa, I am a servant of Rama. I will kill you today." Sugreeva jumped on Ravana, pulled off Ravana's crown and then threw it away. Ravana was shaken and then he catch hold of Sugreeva, threatened him and threw him to the ground. Sugreeva bounced up like a rubber ball and with great strength threw Ravana down. They wrestled with each other for a long time. Ravana understood that it would not be possible to defeat Sugreeva with his strength. He understood that Sugreeva could be defeated only by magical tricks. Sugreeva immediately understood this, withdrew and went back to Rama. Sugreeva felt happy about what he did. All the monkeys too felt happy and showed their happiness by jumping up and down. Rama hugged Sugreeva.

Rama afterwards, smilingly scolded him, "You have done this without asking and taking permission from me. A king should not do such things. The death of a king is a loss for all the people in the kingdom. If Ravana had killed you, I would have immediately killed him."

Thus, Sugreeva then explained his views. "I lost my control when I saw the rogue who stole Seetha and in a fit of anger did this."

Rama consoled him, "What you did is courageous and great. It will be a big boost for the confidence for our army."

Rama came down from the Mountain Suvela and inspected his own army and was happy. Rama took up his bow and arrows and started marching with his army. The monkeys took rocks and trees in their hands and started walking. They thus reached the boundary walls of the palace. Rama took position in the northern gate, Neela with Mainda and Dwivida in the eastern gate, Angada in the southern gate and Hanuman in the western gate. Sugreeva stood in the middle of the fort. Thus, Rama's army surrounded Lanka on all the four sides. Seeing Rama's army of monkeys surrounding the palace boundary walls, the rakshasas were afraid and went back and informed Ravana about this.

Ravana after hearing this, went on top of the palace and closely scrutinised the enemy army. He saw Rama and was confused about what to do. Rama sent Angada as his messenger to meet Ravana. Angada came in front of Ravana who was sitting with his ministers, after jumping over the northern gate. Angada revealed his identity. "My name is Angada, nephew of Sugreeva who is the king of Kishkindha. I have come here as a messenger of Rama. Due to your cruel actions against the munis, all your blessings have disappeared. I have come here to kill you. If you do not surrender and honourably give back Seetha, I will kill you and make Vibheeshana the king."

Ravana was consumed with anger. He ordered the ministers to seize Angada. Four rakshasas caught Angada by his hands and

Angada let them catch him. He considered this as an opportunity to show his strength. When the rakshasas were holding Angada, he jumped to the top of the palace. The rakshasas fell on the ground. Angada destroyed the roof of the palace and went back to Rama. Ravana who saw the strength of Angada sat helplessly with wide open eyes. Ravana felt that his end was nearing.

Rama then ordered the army to kill the rakshasa army. The monkey army, on hearing Rama's orders, started chanting, "May Rama and Lakshmana win the war and be victorious." They took rocks and trees in their hand, then destroyed a part of the boundary wall and entered Lanka. Seeing this, Ravana too ordered his army to start the war. The rakshasas started attacking the monkey army with maces and other weapons. The monkeys fought back. The rakshasas climbed on top of the wall and killed many monkeys. The monkeys pulled down the rakshasas who climbed on top of the wall and killed them. There were lots of dead bodies on the battle field.

Hanuman started fighting with Jambumali, Angada with Indrajith, Neela with Nikumbha and Sugreeva with Prakhasa. All the places were drenched with blood. Indrajith hit Angada with the mace. Angada snatched the mace from Indrajith and destroyed his chariot. Jambumali injured Hanuman. Hanuman jumped on to Jambumali's chariot, and with one big blow killed him. Rama, Lakshmana, Sugreeva and Nala killed many rakshasas. The monkey army commanders caused a lot of destruction to the enemy's side.

The battle continued at night. In the darkness, the rakshasas attacked Rama with arrows. Angada attacked Indrajith, destroyed his chariot and killed his charioteer. An injured Indrajith disappeared from the war front. He had the skill of fighting invisibly with the blessing of Brahma and started sending snake-like arrows at Rama and Lakshmana. These arrows wounded Rama and Lakshmana and they were pinned by a network of those arrows. Rama instructed Hanuman, Neela and Angada to find where Indrajith was. Indrajith then sent arrows at Hanuman and Angada. Indrajith started speaking, unseen by others, "O Rama and Lakshmana, even Indra can't see me. Then how will it be possible for you to see me? My next desire is to kill both of you."

Rama and Lakshmana had arrows all over their body and soon they became unconscious and fell on the ground. The monkeys were very sad and unhappy and stood around Rama and Lakshmana. Seeing this, Indrajith was very happy and thought, "Both Rama and Lakshmana must have died due to the snake arrows. Even Indra can't save them." Hearing this from Indrajith, all the rakshasas were very thrilled and started shouting, "Rama is dead. Indrajith could alone defeat the enemies." Indrajith returned to Ravana's palace.

Rama and Lakshmana who were lying in blood, were hardly able to breath. Sugreeva and Vibheeshana reached there. Vibheeshana tried to console them.

Indrajith reached the palace and informed his father proudly about the victory in the war. Ravana was very happy to know that Rama and Lakshmana were killed. He jumped up, hugged his son Indrajith and asked, "Son, how did you do this almost impossible task alone? Please explain all in detail."

Indrajith answered, "I, unseen by others from the sky attacked Rama and Lakshmana with snake arrows and tied them up. Then I attacked them with arrows and killed them. The monkey army was very sad and stopped the war."

The news about the death of Rama and Lakshmana rid Ravana of all the fears he had about the war. He called all the rakshasis who were guarding Seetha and told them that his son who had no equal in the world had killed Rama and Lakshmana. "Take Seetha in the Pushpaka vimana to the place where the dead bodies of Rama and Lakshmana are lying." After sending the rakshasis, Ravana proclaimed to the people of Lanka about the death of Rama and Lakshmana. After knowing the death of Rama and Lakshmana from the rakshasis, Seetha was very sad, she became unconscious and fell on the ground.

Under the supervision of Trijata, the rakshasis took Seetha in the Pushpaka vimana and took her to the battlefield. The ground was strewn with the dead bodies of rakshasas and monkeys. Seetha saw all this. Then she saw the bodies of Rama and Lakshmana covered with arrows. The monkeys were standing around sorrowfully. She also heard the noise of the victory celebration of the rakshasas. Seetha was very sad and thought that with the death of her husband, all her happiness in the world had come to an end. Trijata then consoled and assured Seetha saying that Rama and Lakshmana were not dead. "You could not have come in the Pushpaka vimana if that was the case. Pay attention to the monkeys. They are not mourning. They are only protecting Rama and Lakshmana. The faces of Rama and Lakshmana are still shining. Seetha, do not unnecessarily worry, they are alive." Seetha felt better, but she was unhappy and sad about the miserable state they were in. She then returned to the Ashoka garden.

Rama by that time had become conscious. Lakshmana was lying in a pool of blood. Rama thought, "If Lakshmana dies, all my effort will go in vain. If Lakshmana dies, I will also take my life. If I allow him to die, how will I face the mothers and look at them?" Rama afterwards instructed Sugreeva, "Withdraw the monkey army and return to Kishkindha. In the absence of me and Lakshmana, our army will be subject to the destructive attack of the rakshasas. I thank all of you for your support with devotion and friendship. I am indebted to you all of you for your courage and devotion to the cause ignoring your lives."

After hearing the sweet words from Rama, tears started falling from the eyes of the monkeys. Vibheeshana arrived there. He gave necessary inspiration to the monkeys. Vibheeshana was upset after seeing the condition of Rama and Lakshmana. Sugreeva consoled Vibheeshana and said, "Rama and Lakshmana will get cured and will be ready for the war. There is no doubt about defeating Ravana."

Sugreeva then instructed Sushena, "Take Rama and Lakshmana to Kishkindha. There they will be safe and will get cured fast also take the complete army also to Kishkindha. I will fight alone, kill Ravana and bring back Seetha."

Sushena then suggested, "Some Medicinal plants can heal them. They are Sanjivakarani and Vishalyakarani. They can cure and heal the wounds. Panasa and Sasathi can identify these plants. It is available in the Mountain Chandra. They will give new life to the patients. Hanuman can travel fast and hence it is advisable to send Hanuman."

Suddenly a mighty wind blew, and the sky was filled with clouds. Waves rose in the sea. Garuda the eagle flew to Rama and Lakshmana. Immediately, the snake arrows binding Rama and Lakshmana flew away. The bird smoothly and gently touched the body of Rama and Lakshmana. Immediately both of them came back to their original state of healthy condition. The bird picked up Rama and hugged him. Rama lovingly asked the bird, "Who are you? We both are indebted to you till our death. Please clarify who you are."

The bird replied, "I am Vinatha's son, Garuda, your co-traveller. Devas or Indra cannot save you from the snake arrows. These snakes are the children of Kadru and they are in the magical cover of Indrajith. Brahma had given this blessing to Indrajith. O Lord, rakshasas are cheats and they have magical power. You have to be careful while fighting with them. I wish you all success in the war and you will be able to take back Seetha."

Garuda went around Rama (did *pradakshina*) and flew away. The monkeys were very happy on seeing Rama and Lakshmana completely healed. They started dancing. They were ready to go to war again. Sounds of the monkeys rejoicing was heard in the palace of Ravana. They assumed that Rama and Lakshmana must have recovered. Ravana sent some rakshasas to the roof of the palace to closely watch the situation. They were surprised to see Rama and Lakshmana, uninjured and healthy. They were afraid and ran back to Ravana and informed all what they saw.

An angry Ravana sent Dhumraksha to attack Rama. Dhumraksha immediately collected the rakshasas and started his march towards the western gate with his donkeys pulling the chariot towards where Hanuman had camped with his monkeys. When he was travelling along the street, he saw many bad omens. But with courage he travelled towards the monkey army. They were standing ready for war. A horrible battle ensued there. The monkey army attacked the rakshasas with rocks, trees and with their nails and teeth. They started tearing the body of the rakshasas by biting and scratching them with their nails. Seeing the courageous war of the monkeys, the rakshasas were driven away. Dhumraksha then started a deadly attack against the monkey army. The monkeys ran away in fright. Hanuman seeing this took a big rock and threw it at Dhumraksha's chariot. The chariot broke into pieces. Hanuman took another rock and attacked Dhumraksha. With the force of the attack, Dhumraksha was killed. Dhumraksha's army was afraid and they decided to withdrew.

Ravana next sent Vajradamshtra. He went to the southern gate where Angada was stationed. There a terrible war between Vajradamshtra and Angada begin by throwing a big rock Angada destroyed the Vajradamshtra's chariot. The next rock hit Vajradamshtra's head and he became unconscious. On waking up, he hit Angada's chest with his mace. Then they started wrestling. After some time, they were tired and had no more strength. Then Vajradamshtra attacked Angada with his sword. Angada took the sword from him and cut off his head. When the captain was killed the rakshasa army ran back.

Ravana next sent Akampana for the war. He told Akampana, "You are well versed and smart in using all type of war weapons. You go and destroy the monkey army, Rama and Lakshmana."

Akampana saw many bad omens on the way. Disregarding them, he proceeded to the battlefield. In the terrible battle that followed between Akampana and Hanuman, the area was covered in dust and they could not see each other. Akampana started showering arrows on Hanuman when he faced him. Hanuman uprooted a mountain and threw it at him. Akampana's arrows shattered it to pieces. Hanuman then uprooted a tree and struck Akampana on the head with it. Akampana fell dead.

After seeing this, Rama and Lakshmana lovingly hugged Hanuman. The death of Akampana disturbed Ravana badly. He then inspected and discussed the security system of Lanka with his ministers. He informed and instructed Prahastha that there were only five people left now capable of facing the monkey army. "They are me, you, Indrajith, Kumbhakarna and Nikumbha."

Prahastha then said, "I was the first person to tell you to return Seetha. But I am prepared to go and fight the war and if required, lose my life for your sake." Prahastha then set out to the battlefield. Vultures, eagles and wolfs were all around the battle field. It was a bad omen. The reigns were falling from the hand of the charioteer. Prahastha felt uneasy. He directed his chariot towards Sugreeva, like the moth falling into the fire. Prahastha showered arrows on Neela and Neela was injured. Ignoring this, Neela took a rock and threw it at Prahastha and his chariot was broken in pieces. Prahastha got down from the chariot, took a mace and attacked Neela. Neela took a big rock and threw it at Prahastha. Its impact broke Prahastha's head and he died. Lakshmana came and congratulated Neela.

Ravana came to know about the death of Prahastha and was very sad about it. He convened a conference of all his ministers and informed them that he himself was going to war. By that time Rama could recognise Ravana. Rama said, "He has a radiant face. I am happy that he has come in front of me. I am going to show my anger towards him."

Ravana marched out of the city and with a roar divided the monkey army in two groups. Sugreeva threw a mountain top at Ravana. Ravana broke that into pieces with his arrows and sent an arrow at Sugreeva. Sugreeva was injured and fell on the floor. Many monkeys were killed by Ravana's arrows. The monkeys then went back and sought refuge with Rama.

Lakshmana wanted to attack Ravana. Rama agreed. Meanwhile Hanuman confronted Ravana. He then told Ravana, "The blessings you had got from Brahma will not save you from the monkeys. My one beating is enough to kill you. How easily I killed your son Akshakumar. Have you forgotten that?"

Ravana hit Hanuman on the chest and Hanuman fell a step back. Hanuman then hit Ravana. Two enemies of equal strength were facing each other. Ravana then turned towards Neela. He injured Neela. Neela started attacking Ravana with rocks and trees. Ravana could stop them all by his arrows. At the end, Ravana sent the Agneyasthra, a fire missile on Neela and he fell unconscious.

Lakshmana arrived at that point and challenged Ravana. They exchanged heated words. Ravana showered arrows on Lakshmana which he could easily stop. Ravana could also stop and prevent all Lakshmana's arrows. Ravana next sent the Brahmasthra at Lakshmana. It hit Lakshmana's forehead and Lakshmana fell on the ground. Lakshmana then sent three arrows which hurt Ravana. Ravana fell down on the ground. Ravana got up with difficulty and threw the arrow, given to him by Brahma at Lakshmana. Lakshmana could not resist the attack of that weapon. That arrow hit Lakshmana on the chest and he fell unconscious on the ground. Ravana tried to carry Lakshmana away. But Lakshmana had prayed to Lord Vishnu. Due to that, Lakshmana's weight increased so much that Ravana could not even lift or move Lakshmana's body.

Ravana then got into his chariot. Hanuman also got into Ravana's chariot and hit him on the chest. Ravana fell on the ground. The monkeys started dancing with happiness and pleasure. Hanuman carried Lakshmana to Rama. Immediately, the arrow which had hit Lakshmana came out and went back to Ravana. The magical power of Lord Vishnu made Lakshmana's injury heal.

Rama then sat on Hanuman's shoulder and went to the battlefield. Ravana was still sitting in his chariot. Ravana with anger attacked Hanuman. Rama with only one arrow destroyed Ravana's chariot. The next arrow of Rama hit Ravana's chest. He fell down unconscious. Rama also destroyed Ravana's flag post. Rama then told Ravana, "Go back and take rest. I am not killing you now as you are injured."

Ravana with his pride shattered, went back lowering his head.

Ravana sadly sat on the seat in the palace and called all his ministers. He then disclosed these things. "When Brahma gave me the boon, he had asked me to be careful about human beings. I was cursed by an Ikshwaku king Anaranya saying that I will be killed by a king from their kingdom along with all relatives. On another occasion, when I lifted the Mount Kailash, Uma had cursed me that my death would be caused by a woman. Once I insulted Nandeeshwar and received a curse from Nandeeshwar that the rakshasas would be destroyed by a monkey army. I was also cursed by Vedavati, Rambha and Punjikasthala. Go quickly and wake up Kumbhakarna. He is our only hope now. He is capable of killing the princes. He is very efficient and courageous."

Many rakshasas went to Kumbhakarna's residence to wake him up. They heaped food in front of him. They applied perfume and fragrant *chandan* on his body. They started singing songs in a loud voice while praising him. He did not wake up. They created a din by beating drums and playing musical instruments but he still did not wake up. They started beating him with maces, attaching nails on it. Still he did not wake up. Then elephants were made to walk all over his body. Then he woke up. He sat up yawning and stretched his hands. He ate all the food placed in front of him.

He was satisfied. He then started shouting at the top of his voice, "Why did you wake me up in this untimely manner? Is there any problem which could not be solved?"

The minister Yuvaksha informed Kumbhakarna, "Rama and Lakshmana have arrived here. They have surrounded the city of Lanka and are attacking us. Many rakshasas including Prince Aksha are dead."

Kumbhakarna then said that he would immediately go and kill Rama and Lakshmana. Then the minister Mahodara suggested that he should meet his brother Ravana first and then take a decision. Some rakshasas went and met Ravana and informed him about Kumbhakarna's waking up and asked Ravana, "Should he directly go and attack Rama and Lakshmana or should he come here, meet you and then take a decision?"

Ravana told them, "Ask Kumbhakarna to come and meet me first. Give him enough food and drink before bringing him here."

When Kumbhakarna went to the palace of Ravana, Rama instructed Neela, "Line up the army at the city gates."

Kumbhakarna then went to meet Ravana. Ravana hugged Kumbhakarna. Kumbhakarna then asked Ravana, "Dear brother, what would I do for you?"

Ravana informed him about Rama and Lakshmana's arrival with the monkey army and the death of many rakshasas. He told Kumbhakarna, "Only you have the capability and strength to kill Rama and Lakshmana."

Kumbhakarna then reminded Ravana about what Vibheeshana and Mandodari had said. "I feel that advice was right. Even now you can give back Seetha and avoid this war. But the final decision lies with you."

Ravana controlled his anger and said, "You should not tell me this when the war is going on. You are the only person who can save us from this sea of war by defeating the enemy."

Kumbhakarna then said, "You need not worry. I will destroy Rama, Lakshmana and the monkey army."

Then minister Mahodara said his opinion, "You have no right to review your brother's decision. He is the king. He has the right to take any decision. You are an egoistic person. It is difficult to defeat Rama."

Mahodara told Ravana, "I will accompany Kumbhakarna to the war. We may win or lose the war. If we lose the war, let us propagate the news that we have won the war. If Seetha knows this information, you can own her promising your good behaviour and a royal life like a princess."

Kumbhakarna angrily said, "What you said is impossible. I will alone go and kill Rama, Lakshmana and the army."

Ravana was very happy. Kumbhakarna went around Ravana (did *pradakshina*). Ravana hugged him and blessed him to win the war.

Thus after meeting Ravana, Kumbhakarna started for the battle. Seeing the colossal Kumbhakarna, the monkeys scattered in fear. Rama was very surprised to see Kumbhakarna. He was seeing for the first time, a rakshasa as huge as a mountain. He asked Vibheeshana, "Who is he?"

Vibheeshana answered, "He is the son of Maharshi Vishravas, Kumbhakarna. He is the biggest among the rakshasas and has even defeated King Yama. He is a very cruel rakshasa. He used to harass the maharshis. He does not get satisfied even on eating big quantities of meat. Even Indra is afraid of Kumbhakarna. Indra once met Brahma and requested him to find a solution for this. Kumbhakarna once received a boon from Brahma. Kumbhakarna asked Brahma the boon of sleeping all the time. Ravana then requested Brahma to alter the boon. Brahma then said that Kumbhakarna would sleep for six months and be awake for a day. He told him to go around the world that day, eat as much food as he can and sleep again for six months. Ravana has woken him up on an emergency breaking his normal sleeping routine. This signifies danger for Kumbhakarna."

After reaching the battlefield, Kumbhakarna saw some bad omens. A big bird came and sat on his flag post. On seeing the colossal Kumbhakarna, the monkeys were frightened and tried to run away. Angada spoke to them, "O brave monkeys, do not rum away. Even though life is dear to us, we must do our duty."

The monkeys attacked Kumbhakarna with rocks and trees. Kumbhakarna killed many monkeys by swallowing them whole. Dwivida threw a big stone at Kumbhakarna which crushed many rakshasas. Kumbhakarna then threw an arrow at Hanuman. Hanuman tried to stop it by a rock but it struck Hanuman on the chest. He fell down, spitting blood. The rakshasas were very happy.

Many monkeys jumped on to the body of Kumbhakarna and bit and scratched him. Kumbhakarna opened his mouth and put them into his mouth and closed it. When Angada saw this, he took a big rock and threw it on Kumbhakarna's head. Kumbhakarna got angry and ran towards Angada. Angada hit Kumbhakarna on the chest and he felt giddy. When he recovered, he struck Angada. Angada became unconscious and fell down.

Kumbhakarna with a thrishul in hand, ran towards Sugreeva. Sugreeva threw a big rock at Kumbhakarna, but it got broken in pieces. Seeing the fight between Kumbhakarna and Sugreeva, Hanuman jumped up and pulled away the weapon from Kumbhakarna, broke it and threw it away. Kumbhakarna got angry, then he took a mountain portion and threw it at Sugreeva. It hit Sugreeva on his chest and he became unconscious. Kumbhakarna carried Sugreeva in his arm and went back to Lanka.

Hanuman knew that when Sugreeva recovered consciousness, he was capable of escaping from the hands of Kumbhakarna. After reaching Lanka, the people greeted Kumbhakarna by spraying perfumed water and giving him dried food grains. When the water spray fell on Sugreeva's face, he became conscious. He wondered how he would escape. He bit Kumbhakarna's ears and nose and tore them. Also, he injured him by biting and scratching him. Kumbhakarna with anger threw Sugreeva on the ground. Sugreeva jumped up and flew away to Rama's place. Kumbhakarna was still hungry. He took a stick with thorns and started catching and eating the monkeys. Lakshmana then led the attack against Kumbhakarna. Kumbhakarna stopped all those arrows and told Lakshmana, "I want to fight with Rama. Where is he?"

Kumbhakarna rushed towards Rama. Rama then sent a special arrow Rudrasthra towards Kumbhakarna. It struck him on his chest. Rama's arrows decimated the weapons in Kumbhakarna's hands. "You are the cruellest among rakshasas. I am going to kill you, come in front of me," Rama said.

Kumbhakarna took his hammer and advanced towards Rama. Rama used the Vayavya asthra to cut off his hand holding the hammer. With more arrows, he chopped off Kumbhakarna's other hand and feet. Kumbhakarna started crawling on the ground towards Rama. Rama sent many arrows into his open mouth, and Kumbhakarna found it difficult to breath. The next arrow cut off Kumbhakarna's head.

Seeing Kumbhakarna dead, the monkeys started praising Rama with songs. Rama also felt happy having done this courageous act. Even the celestials rejoiced. The body of Kumbhakarna fell into to the sea and his head rolled and fell on the palace road.

Ravana fell unconscious after hearing this news. He felt that life without Kumbhakarna was going to be difficult. He also thought that he should have listened to his God-loving brother Vibheeshana.

Thrishirass, son of Ravana consoled him and said that he would now go to war with the special weapons he had got from Brahma. He also took some of his brothers, who were experts in war, namely Devanthaka, Naranthaka and Athikeya and told Ravana, "I am going to destroy Rama, Lakshmana and the monkey army. We all have the capacity to fight from the sky. You need not worry."

These words gave some consolation to Ravana. Ravana garlanded his sons and blessed them for success in the war. He also sent Mahodara and Mahaparshwa to help Thrishirass. They reached the war zone and from both the sides, they shouted challenging each other. In a short time the death toll started increasing, chariots were broken, and trees and rocks were littered around the area.

Naranthaka created havoc amongst the monkey army with his barbed javelin. Sugreeva gave instructions to Angada to face Naranthaka, son of Ravana. Angada challenged Naranthaka, "If you have courage, send the thrishul at me." The thrishul sent by Naranthaka, hit Angada's chest and it was broken. Naranthaka got down from the chariot and a fierce fight ensued between them. Angada saved himself from the attack and kicked Naranthaka on his chest. Naranthaka was killed.

Mahodara could not bear the death of his brother. He along with Devanthaka and Thrishirass marched towards Angada and attacked him. Angada surrounded by all three, fought bravely. Devanthaka hit Angada with his iron rod. When Angada got up, Thrishirass sent three arrows at Angada's forehead. Angada was injured. Neela and Hanuman came to help Angada. In the battle, Hanuman killed Devanthaka and Neela killed Mahodara.

Thrishiras attacked Hanuman with the thrishul. Hanuman caught hold of it and broke it. Thrishirass took his sword and attacked him. In the fight, his sword slipped from his hands. Hanuman quickly picked up the sword from Thrishirass and cut all his three heads and killed him. The monkeys were very happy and started shouting after the win.

In the battle between Mahaparshwa and Rishabha, Mahaparshwa was killed. Just then, a colossal rakshasa on a chariot armed with weapons started attacking the monkey army. The monkeys were afraid and started running back and informed Rama. Rama asked Vibheeshana, "Who is that?"

Vibheeshana said, "He is Ravana's son. He has defeated Indra and Varuna in the war. His name is Athikaya. He has the capability to destroy our monkey army. We should therefore kill him first."

Athikaya went up to Rama and challenged him to fight. Lakshmana was enraged and picked up the bow, which made a resounding noise with its string. Athikaya was a bit startled but told Lakshmana, "You are a boy. Are you in a hurry to die?"

They started fighting. Lakshmana and Athikaya showered arrows on each other. Lakshmana sent the flaming Agneya asthra at Athikaya. Athikaya made it ineffective by using the flaming solar missile. He next used the Aisheeka asthra given by Tvasa, the architect of gods. Lakshmana made it ineffective by using the Indra asthra. Athikaya next sent the Yama asthra. Lakshmana stopped it by using the Vayavya asthra. Vayudeva came at that time and told Lakshmana, "Athikaya has a got blessing from Brahma and therefore it is difficult to defeat him. You have to use only the Brahmasthra against him." Lakshmana then sent the Brahmasthra at Athikaya, which cut off his head. He fell dead on the ground. The rakshasa army sadly ran back to Lanka. The monkeys started dancing around Lakshmana with happiness and joy.

Ravana was very sad after hearing the death of his son Athikaya. He felt that Rama and Lakshmana were very strong. "It will be difficult to defeat them. Rama may be Lord Vishnu in the form of a human being as everybody is saying. I should have believed it and also the fact that it will be impossible for anybody to defeat Rama."

Indrajith consoled his crying father. "You do not have to worry about anything so long as I am there. I will immediately go and finish the lives of Rama and Lakshmana."

After getting the blessings of his father Ravana, Indrajith conducted a *homa* (a type offering in the fire) for the success of the war. Indrajith's chariot was driven by donkeys. He flew to the sky with the chariot. He had a blessing that he could remain unseen. He started attacking the monkeys from there. Monkeys started attacking the unseen enemy with rocks and trees. They could not see Indrajith who was in the sky. Indrajith then sent a Brahmasthra. Thousands of arrows rained down and many monkeys died. Hanuman, Sugreeva, Jambavan and Neela could not face them. They got injured and fell on the ground. Rama and Lakshmana felt helpless.

Rama who was badly injured, told Lakshmana, "Indrajith has sent the Brahmasthra. So long as he is unseen, nobody will be able to defeat him. We have to therefore suffer the attack. When we are unconscious, Indrajith will go and meet Ravana to tell him about his victory in the war."

Indrajith saw Rama and Lakshmana lying unconscious, shouted loudly with happiness and rushed towards Lanka and informed his father about what had happened.

The monkeys were very sad after seeing the unconscious Rama and Lakshmana. Vibheeshana consoled them, "They, as a mark of respect for Brahmasthra have willingly accepted the situation. They will get up shortly and start fighting against the enemy." Hanuman decided to console the remaining monkeys. Hanuman and Vibheeshana with torches in their hands, went around the battlefield and started searching for their friends. Sugreeva, Angada, Neela and Nala and other monkey captains were lying on the ground due to attack of the Brahmasthra.

Jambavan had the maximum injuries and he had almost lost his vision. Jambavan first asked, "Is Hanuman alive?"

Vibheeshana asked Jambavan, "Why are you not asking about Rama, Lakshmana, Sugreeva and Angada? Why are you only asking about Hanuman?"

Jambavan said, "If Hanuman is alive, even the dead army monkeys are safe." After hearing this, Hanuman bowed, and touched Jambavan's feet and informed him that he was safe.

After that, Jambavan gave instructions to Hanuman, "Go to the Mountain Himalaya and find the Mountain Oushadi (Mahodaya). It is a shining mountain in the Himalayas. There are good medicinal plants available there. The Mritasanjeevani which can bring back the lives of the people, the Vishalyakarani which can heal wounds, the Sauvarnakarani which can remove the scars due to wounds and the Sandhanakarani, which can join the broken joints. You must pluck all of them and return immediately. We can bring back to life all the monkeys who have died."

Hanuman immediately decided to take up this assignment. He climbed up to the Mountain Thrikuda, enlarged his body, pressed his feet on the ground, jumped into the sky and started flying. Hanuman reached the Himalayas. He saw the Mountain Oushadi. Hanuman could see the illumination from the medicinal plants. Once he got down on the mountain, he could not make out the medicinal plants but knew where they were growing on the mountain. Hanuman picked up the portion of the mountain containing those plants and flew back to Lanka and got down on the Mountain Thrikuda. The monkeys who saw this were extremely happy and started jumping up and down with joy. Using the medicines, the injuries were treated. After treating everybody of the injuries, Hanuman went to the Himalayas with the mountain portion, placed it in its original location and came back to Lanka. Hanuman did all these wonderful deeds in one single day.

Sugreeva then gave a suggestion, "Many rakshasas have died in the war and also many sons of Ravana. They are therefore grieving and will not be on alert. We should therefore attack Lanka tonight with the required lamps and lights."

Immediately, the monkey army started moving towards Lanka. The rakshasas started running away after seeing the monkey army. The monkeys set fire to buildings, streets and gates. The residents of Lanka ran away, fearing for their lives. Rama drew his bow and a tremendous sound issued from it. With his arrows, Rama destroyed the main gate of the city.

This made Ravana very angry. He immediately deputed Kumbhakarna's two sons Kumbha and Nikumbha to face and fight against Rama. He also sent the army captains Yupaksha, Shonithaksha, Prajangha and Kampana to help them in the war. The war continued after that and it was very terrible. Angada first killed Kampana and then Prajangha. Yupaksha and Shonithaksha started fighting with Mainda and Dwivida. Dwivida cut Shonithaksha's face with his nails and threw him to the floor, kicked him and killed him. Mainda crushed Yupaksha's body with his bare hands and killed him. Kumbha attacked and injured Mainda and Dwivida. Angada fought with Kumbha. Angada became unconscious due to his injuries. The monkeys informed Rama about it. Rama sent Jambavan and Sugreeva to help Angada.

Sugreeva fought with Kumbha and told him, "You are tired now. I can kill you. You go back to Lanka and come back later. We can fight afterwards." Kumbha was not ready to listen to the words of Sugreeva. Kumbha caught hold of Sugreeva and started squeezing his body. Both started fighting. Sugreeva took Kumbha and threw him to the sea. Kumbha got up and resumed fighting Sugreeva. Sugreeva then dealt Kumbha a massive blow on the chest. Kumbha died and fell down.

Nikumbha after seeing the death of his brother, came forward to fight with Hanuman. He hit Hanuman with an iron club on the chest. The club was shattered in pieces. Finally, Hanuman killed Nikumbha.

Ravana then sent son of Khara, Makaraksha for the war Maharaksha saw many bad omens on the way. Ignoring them, he proceeded to the battle. Makaraksha and his army attacked the monkeys with swords, spears, arrows and many other weapons. The monkeys fled from the attack. Rama on seeing this sent arrows at Maharaksha. Maharaksha fought back. In the continuing war, Makaraksha got hit by Rama's Agneya asthra and was killed. Seeing this, the rakshasas ran back to Lanka.

Ravana asked Indrajith to go to the battlefield. Indrajith under cover of invisibility, attacked them and many monkeys were killed. Rama and Lakshmana could not see Indrajith. Rama told Lakshman that they would have to defeat Indrajith by divine weapons. Indrajith guessed Rama's intentions and returned to Lanka.

After some time, the monkeys were shocked to see Indrajith on his chariot with Seetha. They did not realise that it was only an illusion. The monkeys looked on helplessly as Indrajith pulled Seetha's hair. Then pulling out a sword, Indrajith killed a crying Seetha. He then told Hanuman, "All your efforts to rescue Seetha have gone in vain." Hanuman informed Rama about what had happened.

Rama became unconscious after hearing this. The monkeys sprinkled water on his face. Lakshmana took Rama in his hands and started crying. He thought, "Is evil triumphing over virtue? I will immediately go and destroy Lanka and Ravana."

At that time, Vibheeshana arrived. On seeing the grief-stricken Lakshmana and the unconscious Rama, he asked, "What happened?"

Lakshmana said, "The evil Indrajith has killed Seetha."

Vibheeshana interrupted, "I know Ravana very well. He would never agree to kill Seetha. Indrajith, by the art of illusion, has made us believe that Seetha is killed. So do not get worried. Lakshmana, you must immediately go to the place called Nikumbhila where Indrajith is doing a fire *homa*. If he completes that, he can again fight unseen by others. You have to go and obstruct that *homa* and kill him by attacking him. When Brahma was giving the boon of divine arms and horses with wings to Indrajith, Brahma had told him that he would be killed in Nikumbhila by the enemy before he completed the *homa*."

Rama immediately asked Lakshmana to go to Nikumbhila and attack Indrajith. He also sent Vibheeshana and Hanuman along with the army to help Lakshmana. Lakshmana bowed to Rama, touched his feet and took the oath that he would kill Indrajith and then he proceeded to Nikumbhila. Vibheeshana asked Lakshmana to attack the rakshasas. “When they are in difficulty, Indrajith will become visible and come to help them. He will go to offer oblations for the *homa*. At that time you must kill him.”

Lakshmana started attacking the rakshasa army. Indrajith who was doing the *homa* had to stop. He soon arrived on his chariot. On seeing Vibheeshana, Indrajith got angry and told him, “My own father’s brother is helping the enemy to kill me. You have no love for the family and you are a traitor. You are siding with the enemies and trying to destroy the family.”

Vibheeshana then said, “I was born as a rakshasa. But I am not cruel or egoistic and have good moral habits. Your father is cruel and arrogant. Stealing another’s wife is a hateful act. You are supporting your father in that. You are very egoistic, cruel and foolish. At last Lakshmana is going to kill you.”

A terrible war ensued between Lakshmana and Indrajith. They showered arrows on each other. Indrajith sent a divine asthra given to him by Yama. Lakshmana stopped it with a divine asthra given to him by Kubera. The arrows collided with each other, making an explosive noise and light. Lakshmana next used the Varuna asthra. Indrajith stopped it by using the Rudra asthra. Indrajith then sent the Agneya asthra at Lakshmana. Lakshmana stopped it by using the Surya asthra. Indrajith angrily used the Asura asthra on Lakshmana. Many weapon like thrishuls, swords, maces and wheels started coming issuing from that. Lakshmana could face them without difficulty with the Maheshwara asthra. Indrajith had by that time the fear of failing in war and it disturbed him mentally. Understanding the difficult situation of Indrajith, Lakshmana then sent the Indra asthra which nobody could stop. This cut off Indrajith’s head. The monkeys were very happy and started dancing with joy and shouting.

Vibheeshana, Hanuman and Jambavan congratulated Lakshmana on his victory. The injured Lakshmana was carried to Rama by Vibheeshana and Hanuman supporting him on their shoulders. Rama expressed his regards first for Lakshmana. Vibheeshana explained to Rama how Lakshmana killed Indrajith, in detail. Rama was extremely happy and said, "Indrajith was killed after three days of war. Now Ravana will come to war himself."

Rama asked Sushena to treat Lakshmana. Sushena gave a medicinal plant to Lakshmana to smell. Lakshmana recovered from his injuries and had no more pain. Lakshmana was extremely happy.

Ravana's Death

Ravana's ministers informed him about the killing of Indrajith by Lakshmana with the support of Vibheeshana. Ravana became unconscious. When he recovered, he was struck with grief. Then he was consumed with anger. All the rakshasas on seeing him, ran away in fear. He took the bow and arrow given to him by Brahma and went to the Ashoka garden. He said, "I am going to kill Seetha now." Many ministers accompanied him. They tried to dissuade him, but he did not agree.

On seeing the enraged Ravana, Seetha thought, "He may not be able to kill Rama and Lakshmana, and therefore came to kill me."

His minister, Suparshwa, advised Ravana, "You know the Vedas well and you follow all rituals and hence it is not at all correct and is immoral to kill an ordinary woman. Use your anger and strength to fight with Rama and Lakshmana and kill them; do not kill a woman. If you can kill Rama and Lakshmana, Seetha will be yours."

These suggestions were acceptable to Ravana. He went back to the palace. He sent the remaining rakshasa army to fight against Rama and Lakshmana. "If they can't kill them, I will go myself," he thought.

A big war ensued between the rakshasas and the monkeys. Many monkeys were killed. The monkeys went to Rama for refuge. Rama then used the Gandharva asthra and he became unseen by others. With the bright light of the Gandharva asthra, a thousand Ramas were seen in the sky. Rama destroyed or killed about two lakh rakshasas fighting from the ground, eighteen thousand elephant-riding rakshasas, fourteen thousand horse-riding rakshasas and many chariot-riding rakshasas with his Gandharva asthra. The devas from the sky praised Rama. The surviving rakshasas ran back in fear to Lanka. Rama told Hanuman, Sugreeva and Vibheeshana, "Only Lord Siva and I can use the Gandharva asthra."

Meanwhile, Lanka was filled with the cries of the rakshasis who had lost their husbands in battle. They all blamed Shoorpanakha for starting the war. "How could that hideous Shoorpanakha expect Rama to marry her? For her sake, our king, Ravana has created enmity with the mighty Rama. If Ravana had listened to Vibheeshana's advice, Lanka would not be a burial ground now. There is no hope for us."

Ravana became very angry on hearing the cries of the widows. He immediately left for the battlefield in a chariot driven by eight horses. He placed all the divine arms in the chariot. With songs of resounding success and the blowing of conches, he started for the war. The monkey army was afraid after hearing these sounds. The clouds covered the sky. A vulture came and sat on his flag post. There were many bad omens.

Ravana despite all this started the war courageously. He created a lot of destruction and death in the monkey army. He challenged Sugreeva to fight. Sugreeva fought with the rakshasas. Virupaksha seated on an elephant attacked Sugreeva. Sugreeva pulled out a tree and threw it at the elephant of Virupaksha. The elephant and Virupaksha fell down. Virupaksha attacked Sugreeva with a sword. Sugreeva got up and kicked Virupaksha on his chest and then gave him a massive blow on the temple. Virupaksha fell down dead. Ravana then sent Mahodara who too was killed by Sugreeva. Mahaparshwa was killed by Angada in battle.

On seeing the death of all his ministers, Ravana vowed to kill Rama. He employed the Tamasa missile on the monkeys. The monkey army was driven away as they could not withstand this missile. Rama and Lakshmana then confronted Ravana. Lakshman aimed arrows at Ravana but Ravana struck down all his arrows. Ignoring Lakshmana, Ravana confronted Rama.

A terrific battle ensued between Rama and Ravana. The sky was covered with arrows from both sides. The rakshasa army and monkey army stopped their war and started watching the battle between Rama and Ravana. Ravana sent many arrows aimed at Rama's forehead which Rama stopped by the Rudra asthra. Ravana next sent the Asura asthra. Arrows with the heads of lions, tigers and snakes went towards Rama. Rama faced them with the

Agneya asthra. The Agneya asthra burnt them half way on their path. But many monkeys were killed. Ravana next sent the Rudra asthra given to him by Maya. Clubs and maces came forward, blazing, along with thunderbolts. Rama made them ineffective by his Gandharva asthra. Ravana next sent the Surya asthra. Blazing discuses issued from that. The sky was lit. Rama with cleverness stopped all of them.

Ravana sent an arrow towards Rama's right shoulder. Rama stopped it. Lakshmana then destroyed Ravana's flag post, cut it in pieces, killed his charioteer and broke his bow. Vibheeshana killed Ravana's horses. Ravana got down from his chariot, came down and threw a thrishul at Vibheeshana. Lakshmana with his arrows cut the thrishul in pieces. Ravana became impatient and threw another thrishul at Lakshmana. Lakshmana fell down unconscious. Rama was sad and pulled out the thrishul from Lakshmana's body. He asked Hanuman and Sugreeva to take care of Lakshmana.

Now Rama was ready for the last battle with Ravana. He was determined to kill the cruel rakshasa. Ravana was not able to withstand the attack. He ran back from the war zone. Sushena told Rama, "Lakshmana's face looks bright. His eyes are shining. Hanuman should immediately go to Mountain Mahodaya and bring the divine plant medicines Sanjeevani, Vishalyakarani, Sauvarnakarani and Sandhanakarani." Hanuman reached the mountain and brought back the medicinal herbs. Sushena could identify these medicines. He prepared the medicines and gave them to Lakshmana through the nose. Lakshmana healed from all of his injuries. Rama said that he was lucky to get Lakshmana alive and healthy. After hearing this Lakshmana asked Rama to get ready for the war.

Ravana came to the battlefield in a new chariot. Rama started showering arrows on Ravana. The devas who were seeing the war felt that the opponents were not on an equal footing.

Ravana was fighting riding on a chariot. Rama was fighting standing on the ground. Indra after seeing this, sent his chariot with his charioteer Matali to Rama. The chariot was a divine golden one. It stopped in front of Rama. Matali requested Rama to accept the chariot. "There are many divine arms of Indra in this and also his special bow and arrow. Please therefore accept this and climb on this chariot." Rama went around the divine chariot (*pradakshina*) and climbed on to the chariot.

The final battle of Rama and Ravana now began. Ravana sent the Gandharva asthra at Rama and Rama stopped it by the same weapon. Ravana next sent the Rakshasa asthra at Rama. The arrows turned into poisonous snakes. Rama stopped them by the Garuda asthra. These arrows turned into eagles and destroyed the snakes. Ravana started showering arrows on Matali and the chariot. He broke the flag post of the chariot. The rakshasa army started shouting and encouraging Ravana. Ravana told Rama to be ready to die. Ravana sent a thrishul by swinging it at Rama. The thrishul approached Rama blazing with fire. Rama took the thrishul from the chariot and threw it at Ravana's thrishul. It broke Ravana's thrishul into pieces. The war continued. Both Ravana and Rama sustained injuries.

Rama told Ravana, "You are a coward to steal Seetha. Your end is nearing."

Rama's arrows injured Ravana very badly and he was in a helpless situation. Understanding the situation, Ravana's charioteer drove away the chariot. When Ravana became alright, he scolded his charioteer for taking the chariot away and instructed him to take the chariot back to Rama.

Agastya muni came there at that time there and met Rama. Rama bowed to Agastya muni. Agastya muni taught him the Adithyahridaya mantra (divine words). He told Rama to recite that mantra and start the war. "Your success in such a case is certain."

When Rama recited the mantra, Suryadeva came in front of him and told him, "Do not delay. Go and start the war."

Rama asked Matali to carefully take the chariot near Ravana. Matali very carefully took the chariot near Ravana and stopped it. The battle was renewed between them. Ravana tried to cut off the flag and flag post of Indra's chariot and Rama stopped it by his arrows. Next Ravana attacked the horses of Indra's chariot. Ravana could not do anything to the chariot as it had divine power. Ravana was furious. He then sent many missiles and arrows with the aid of magic. Rama stopped all of them in time with his arrows. Rama injured Ravana's horses with his arrows.

Rama chopped off one of Ravana's heads with his arrow. The head grew back. Even after Rama had chopped off a hundred heads of Ravana, he was alive. Rama was very much surprised. That time charioteer Matali reminded Rama of the Brahmasthra. "The final time has arrived and you have to use it now." Rama recited Adithyahridaya mantra which was told to him by Agastya muni and with prayer he sent the Brahmasthra at Ravana. It had the bright light of the sun and the fire power of Suryadeva and Agnideva. It pierced Ravana's chest and he died. It came back and sat in Rama's quiver.

The success of Rama was a divine experience for all the monkeys. The rakshasas left the battlefield and ran back to Lanka. The killing of Ravana brought relief, peace and happiness to all devas and rishis. The atmosphere became calm and a cool breeze started blowing. Sugreeva, Angada, Vibheeshana and Lakshmana and many came to congratulate and show their respects to Rama. But Vibheeshana was crying because of the death of his elder brother Ravana.

The information about the death of Ravana reached the palace. Ravana's wives started crying with unbearable sorrow. Some said with sorrow, "You did not listen to your brother Vibheeshana and that is why you had to suffer and die like this. This is a punishment for you for bringing Seetha without her permission."

Ravana's favourite wife Mandodari said, "You were very strong. But you could not recognise Rama with a divine power who is an avathar of Lord Vishnu. You were a fearsome person who stole Seetha. You got into this situation as a result of the sins you have committed. Still, I do not know how I will live without you."

Mandodari fell unconscious on Ravana's body. All the wives made her sit up and revived her. Rama told Vibheeshana to do the required last rites for Ravana and to console his widows. Vibheeshana was not prepared to do the last rites for Ravana.

Vibheeshana said, "I can't do the last rites of a person who was an immoral person."

Rama told him, "That is not right. You should forget everything after the death. It is our duty to do the last rites of your elder brother. Whatever drawbacks Ravana had, he was a courageous warrior."

Vibheeshana agreed and started preparation for the last rites of Ravana. He brought Ravana's mother's father Malyavan. The dead body of Ravana was kept in a chariot and brought out of the war zone. They did the last rites of burning the body in a divine place with all rakshasas including reciting mantras from Vedas and other rituals connected with it. After the function was over Vibheeshana went and consoled all the wives and sent them to the palace.

Rama gave up his anger and was in a composed and calm state of mind. He kept his bow, arrows and quiver, and protective armour on the floor. He gave necessary respect to Matali, Indra's charioteer and gave him permission to go back. Matali got into the chariot and went back to Indra. Rama then asked Lakshmana to make Vibheeshana the king of Lanka by crowning him as the king with the required rituals. It was conducted as specified in the Vedas. All the rakshasas were present for the ceremony. They gave lot of gifts to Vibheeshana. Vibheeshana presented all these items in front of Rama.

Rama sent Hanuman to inform Seetha about the killing of Ravana. The message Rama sent was like this: "You have spent many sleepless nights and now I have done the act of killing Ravana to save you and have kept my promise. Now you should not have any worries." Seetha was very happy to hear it and in a glad mood. She told Hanuman that his message was very precious. Hanuman then told Seetha, "If it is acceptable to you, I can kill all the rakshasis who have troubled you. I feel like taking revenge on them. I am only waiting for your approval."

Seetha then said, "They were the poor servants of the king and were working according to the orders they received. Bad things should not be met by bad ways."

While returning, Hanuman asked Seetha what message he should convey to Rama. She said, "I am eagerly waiting to see my beloved husband." Hanuman returned, promising Seetha that he would make arrangements for her to see Rama and Lakshmana.

Hanuman informed Rama about his meeting with Seetha and her message to him. Tears started flowing from the eyes of Rama. He instructed Vibheeshana to bring Seetha after a special bath and with divine ornaments and clothes. Vibheeshana reached Ashoka garden and informed Seetha about what Rama had said. "I have brought divine ornaments and clothes. We can go in the chariot. Please get ready."

Seetha first said that she wanted to see Rama and then only she would take a bath. Vibheeshana asked Seetha, "Is it not proper for you to obey your husband?"

Seetha agreed. Then bathed and dressed in silk garments and adorned in jewels, she got into the chariot and stood in front of Rama. Rama was seated with an indifferent expression. Seetha after seeing the most beautiful face of Rama forgot all her sorrows and her face started shining like a moon. Rama said, "I have already carried out the promise given to you and I have killed Ravana. That was not for your sake but for the good name of the Ikshwaku family. I do not have any happiness after seeing you. I can't accept a woman who has lived in another's house.

You can go anywhere you like. You can live in the protection of Lakshmana or Bharata."

Seetha for the first time was hearing such cruel words from Rama. Seetha cried for some time, wiped her tears and told Rama, "If this was your plan, you should have informed me this through Hanuman. I would have taken my life. It would not have caused such a big war and the death of many monkeys and rakshasas. Is it the way you give importance to my love, prayers and divine character?"

Seetha instructed Lakshmana, "Make a pyre for me. My husband has declared that I am not acceptable to him in front of an assembly of people. The only way left for me is to jump in the fire."

Lakshmana looked at Rama. Rama did not give any reply. Lakshmana therefore went to prepare the fire as instructed by Seetha. When the fire was burning, Seetha came to Rama, went around in *pradakshina* and approached the fire. She prayed to all devas and Agnideva. She said to Agnideva, "I have not done any bad things by actions or words and have been declared as unclean. I request you to prove my cleanliness."

Walking around the fire, she then entered the fire. The spectators were aghast and surprised. She was consumed by the fire. All the rakshasas and monkeys were very sad. All the devas came in front of Rama. Mahadeva, Indra and Brahma were also present. Rama stood in front of them with folded hands.

They expressed their views as follows, "O Rama, we feel sorry and sad for your ignoring your own beloved wife. You are a god but behave like a common man."

Rama said in grief, "I identify as a man. Tell me who I am."

Brahma reminded Rama that he is another form of Lord Vishnu and Seetha was Mahalakshmi. Seetha then came out of the fire, borne on the hands of Agnideva. Seetha's ornaments, silk sari and body were untouched by fire.

Agnideva told Rama, "Here is your beloved wife Seetha. She has not been affected by any sins; she is clean and divine. Please stop your cruel words and actions against her."

Rama was happy and tears of happiness started flowing from his eyes. He told Agnideva, "I was forced to do this just to make the people believe my sincerity. Otherwise people would cast aspersions on Seetha. I am doing this only to make the people understand me. I and Seetha are not actually separate, we are one. She is my inner strength. I can't give her up."

Rama was extremely and divinely happy with reuniting with Seetha. Mahadeva told Rama, "You have killed Ravana who was considered as extremely strong and unconquerable by anybody and the world will therefore forever remember and praise you."

With the help of Indra, Dasaratha appeared in the sky and told Rama, "My mind was deeply hurt when you were sent to the forest by Kaikeyi. Now you go and rule Ayodhya with Bharata."

Rama requested Dasaratha to withdraw all the bad words he had used against Kaikeyi and Bharata. Dasaratha agreed to that. Then Dasaratha told Lakshmana, "My beloved son, your devoted service for Rama makes me extremely happy. You must have known that your brother is another form of Lord Vishnu." Dasaratha told Seetha, "Do not feel bad about Rama testing your devotion. Your devotion to your husband and your divine quality will become extremely famous." Saying all the above Dasaratha disappeared.

Rama requested Indra to bless and enliven all the dead monkeys and make their dwelling place full with trees, flowers and fruits. Indra said, "It will be difficult to give such a blessing. Since you have asked for it, I am happily agreeing." After that all the devas and Indra disappeared.

Vibheeshana requested Rama to remain there for few days, enjoying all kingly and palace facilities and comforts. Rama told Vibheeshana to give all such facilities to the monkeys and Sugreeva. Rama reminded Vibheeshana that he had to immediately reach Bharata and told him to make arrangements for their return journey. Vibheeshana then gave Rama the happy news that he had already arranged for the Pushpaka vimana for their return to Ayodhya. "This is the plane Ravana had forcefully taken from Kubera. It is made of gold and diamonds are embedded on it. It was constructed by Viswakarma. It has the capability to travel in the sky as per the requirements of the traveller." Rama and Lakshmana were spellbound and surprised by this message. Rama requested Vibheeshana to give gold ornaments to all the monkeys.

Rama Returning to Ayodhya

Rama got into the vimana and told the monkeys, "I do not have anything to give you as compensation for the steady courage and devotion of your duty during the war. Your good name will always be remembered. Now you all go to Kishkindha and live happily under the good rule of Sugreeva." He told Vibheeshana to take over the reins of Lanka immediately. "The people are like orphans now in the absence of a king."

Sugreeva and Vibheeshana requested Rama to take them with him to Ayodhya. "We will come back after seeing your crowning ceremony."

Rama happily agreed for that and said, "I am very happy that you are coming with us. Let many rakshasas and monkeys also come with us."

Thus, the Pushpaka vimana flew to the sky. Rama showed Seetha the places where Ravana, Kumbhakarna, Indrajith and

Prahastha died during the war. He also showed Seetha the sea bridge Sethu. On the other side, he showed the place where Lord Shiva appeared in front of him before starting the construction of the bridge. When they reached Kishkindha, Seetha requested Rama to take the wives of the monkeys also with them. Rama agreed. The plane stopped there accordingly, took the wives of the monkeys and started the onward journey to Ayodhya. Rama showed Seetha many places during the air travel, including the Mountain Rishyamukha, River Godavari, Agastya ashram, Mountain Chithrakoot, River Yamuna, River Ganga, and Guha's kingdom. They also saw all the places they had stayed in during the time of exile and remembered the past.

Rama stopped the plane and got down in Bharadwaja's ashram. The muni received Rama with a very warm welcome. Rama bowed to the muni. Bharadwaja muni had with his divine power known everything about Rama and Bharata. He told Rama, "I am very happy that you have reduced the difficulties on the earth by killing Ravana. Bharata is ruling the country well as an ascetic, abandoning his royal lifestyle, keeping your wooden slippers on the throne as a mark of respect for you. I too am very happy. You can ask me for any blessing that you desire."

Rama requested the muni to bless them by allowing all the trees on both sides of the way to Ayodhya to bloom with flowers and fruits. It happened like that with the blessing of Bharadwaj muni. This was meant for the monkeys. Rama told Hanuman to inform Guha about their arrival and also to go to Nandigram and inform Bharata about all what had happened. Hanuman took the shape of a man and started his journey. He travelled in air and reached Guha's place and communicated to him all what had happened.

When he reached Nandigram, he saw Bharata in a weak state due to his life as an ascetic eating fruits and nuts. He told Bharata, "I am the messenger of Rama. Rama will be reaching Ayodhya very soon and I have come here to inform you that." Bharata was so happy and excited after hearing this news that he became unconscious. After recovering, he hugged Hanuman. "Since you have brought such happy news, I will give ten thousand cows, hundred villages and some more as a gift." He requested Hanuman to sit down and describe in detail what all had happened.

Hanuman described everything and also revealed his identity and name. Bharata was very happy. Bharata instructed Shatrughna to construct a new road to Ayodhya and make all the arrangements to welcome Rama. Sumanthra came riding on top of an elephant. Koushalya, Kaikeyi and Sumithra travelled on chariots and reached Nandigram. All arrangements had been completed.

Bharata took the wooden slippers of Rama and placing it on his head, waited for the arrival of Rama.

Dust flew in the sky, indicating the arrival of the monkeys. They could now see the Pushpaka vimana in the distance. The people on the horsebacks and chariot got down as a mark of respect. The divine Pushpaka vimana then landed. Bharata got inside the vimana and bowed to Rama. Ram hugged Bharata warmly with love and affection. Bharata after that, bowed to Lakshmana and Seetha.

Bharata hugged Sugreeva and told him, "You are a brother to all four of us."

Rama went to Koushalya and fell at her feet and greeted her. He also greeted and bowed to Sumithra, Kaikeyi and Vasishta.

Bharata then took the wooden slippers, walked towards Rama and carefully put them on Rama's feet and told him, "In your absence, the army and our financial position improved considerably. I have carried out my duties and now I am handing over everything to you."

Rama sent back the Pushpaka plane to Kubera. Bharata requested Rama to occupy the auspicious chair meant for the king with all pride and pomp. Rama cut his hair and dressed like a king. The three mothers dressed up Seetha and the female monkeys. Sumanthra arrived in a beautiful chariot. Bharata was driving the chariot, Shatrughna held the specially decorated umbrella and Lakshmana and Vibheeshana stood on both sides of Rama. The devas and rishis sang songs praising Rama from the sky. The monkeys travelled on the backs of elephants. The people had thronged along the sides of the roads to have a look at their beloved king. They started jumping up and down, dancing at the inspiring sight of the young prince. All types of musical instruments, including drums were played. The city was very noisy but happy. The reciting of mantras by Brahmins was also heard. Arrangement was made in the palace for Sugreeva to stay there.

Jambavan, Hanuman, Vegadarshi and Rishabha brought water from five hundred rivers for the crowning ceremony. Nala, Gavavya, Sushena and Rishabha brought water from the four oceans. Vasishta asked Seetha and Rama to sit on a throne studded with precious stones. Vasishta muni with the help of many munis like Vamadeva, Jabali, Kashyapa, Katyayana, Suyajna, Gouthama and Vijaya conducted the crowning ceremony which included pouring of divine water on Rama's head. While Rama was seated on the throne, Vasishta placed the crown on his head. Vayudeva gave Rama a golden ornament chain with a hundred lotus flowers.

After the crowning ceremony, Rama distributed gifts to all the people and Brahmins. Rama gave Sugreeva a golden chain embedded with diamonds, and golden bangles embedded with diamonds to Angada. Rama gave Seetha a beautiful pearl necklace and many dresses. Seetha with the permission of Rama gave the golden ornament given to her by Rama to Hanuman. All monkeys also were given special ornaments and dresses.

❑

Chapter 7
Uthara Kanda

Many rishis had come to see the crowning ceremony of Rama. Uthara Kanda includes Agastya muni explaining to Rama the birth and stories of all rakshasas, Rama sending Seetha to Valmiki's ashram, the birth of Lava and Kusha, the Ashwamedha yaga and the last days of Rama.

Many rishis had come to Ayodhya to witness the crowning ceremony of Rama. Vasishta, Kashyapa, Athri, Viswamitra, Gouthama, Jamadagni, Bharadwaja, Koushik, Kanwa, Agastya, Dhoumya and many others had come. Rama welcomed them with all due respect. They said, "We all are indebted to you because you have killed the following rakshasas who were a great threat to the whole world like Ravana, Kumbhakarna, Khara, Mareecha, Athikaya, Nikumbha, Kumbha and Indrajith. Indrajith who had no equals could only be killed by you and Lakshmana."

After that Agastya muni explained the origin of the rakshasas.

Vishravas was the son of Pulasthya muni and daughter of Thrinabindu rishi. Vishravas had a son named Vishravana with Bharadwaja muni's daughter. He was later known as Kubera. The title Kubera and Pushpaka vimana were given to him by Brahma. After that, Lanka which was specially constructed by Viswakarma for the rakshasas was also given to him. Vishravas had another wife named Kaikesi. Kaikesi was the daughter of Sumali who was from the rakshasa tribe. Their first son called Dashagreeva had ten heads and twenty hands, and was an abnormally sized child. He was later known as Ravana. Their second son was Kumbhakarna, who was a giant even as a child. Their third child was a daughter named Shoorpanakha who was hideous in appearance. Their fourth son was Vibheeshana.

One day, Kubera went to see his father Vishravas. That day Kaikesi desired that her son Ravana also should be beautiful and strong like Kubera. Ravana prayed to Brahma and got a blessing that he couldn't be killed by nagas, rakshasas, and devas. He could be killed by human beings, but Ravana considered them to be inferior to him. Vibheeshana also prayed to Brahma. He wanted a blessing that his mind should not move away from justice and good deeds and was awarded that. While Kumbhakarna asked for a boon, Goddess Saraswathi entered his mouth so that he would ask for a foolish boon. He thus got a blessing to sleep for six months, wake for one day, eat as much as he wants and again go to sleep for six months.

Kaikesi's father Sumali came and met Ravana and asked him to forcibly take over Lanka and Pushpaka vimana. Ravana first refused, saying that it was not good to steal from the elder brother. But Prahastha, Sumali's son, Ravana's maternal uncle persuaded him to take over Lanka and changed Ravana's mind. Ravana had asked Vishravas to give Lanka and Pushpaka vimana to him, but Vishravas was not prepared to do so. Vishravas had understood the cruel mind and egoism of Ravana and requested Kubera to leave Lanka and go to the Mount Kailash.

The Curses on Ravana

Ravana found pleasure in mentally and physically harassing all devas and rishis. Kubera sent a messenger to him, warning him that if he persisted in his evil actions, he would be destroyed. Ravana in anger, went to wage war with Kubera in the Mount

Kailash. Ravana fought with Kubera where Kubera was injured. Kubera was carried away to safety by some rishis. Ravana took the Pushpaka vimana and flew around the world with it. Once, Ravana flew the plane to the Himalayas. The plane could not move forward from there. Nandikeshwara appeared before Ravana and told him that Shankar was relaxing on the mountain and could not be disturbed.

Ravana asked Nandikeshwara, "Who is your Shankar? When I look, all I can see is someone with a monkey-like figure holding a thrishul in hand."

Nandikesha got angry after hearing the insult to Shankar. He then told Ravana, "I can kill you now. But I am not doing that. Since you insulted Lord Shankar in this form, I curse you that you will be killed by monkeys."

Ravana pretended not to hear anything and told Nandikeshwara that he would destroy his master. Ravana with his both hands tried to lift the Himalayas and it started shaking. Parvathi got afraid. Lord Shiva just pressed the mountain down with his toe. Ravana's hands were crushed beneath the mountain. Ravana cried out with pain. His cry even reached the devas and they were afraid. Ravana got the name Ravana (he who makes the world cry) after his terrible cry. Ravana then prayed to Lord Shiva. Shiva was pleased and released his hands.

On his journey through the Himalayas, he came across a very beautiful lady wearing antelope-skin. Ravana asked her, "Who are you?"

She said, "I am the daughter of Kushadhwaja rishi and my name is Vedavati. My father has decided that I will only be married to Lord Vishnu. The Daithya king Shambhu who knew this killed my father when he was sleeping. My mother died by jumping in the cremation fire of my father. I am living in this forest by praying and meditating on Narayana. I know everything about you from my meditative knowledge. Please go away from here."

Ravana pulled her by her hair. Vedavati then transformed her hand into a sword and cut off her hair. As she was touched by Ravana, she entered the fire and took her life. At that time, a shower of flowers fell from heaven. With her meditative power Vedavati reached King Janaka's ploughing land. King Janaka got a child while ploughing the land. Thus, Vedavati born in Sathyayuga became Seetha in the Threthayuga.

Ravana in course of his travel reached Ayodhya. He challenged Ayodhya king Anaranya. In the war that followed, King Anaranya was killed by Ravana. Before dying the king cursed Ravana, saying that a person named Rama from the Ikshwaku family would kill him in future.

Ravana attacked kings, rishis and devas and defeated them in the war. He carried away their daughters and wives. All of them cursed Ravana saying, "O cruel rakshasa, the cause of your death will be a woman." Ravana's capability and brightness started diminishing after the curses. In another war, he killed his sister Shoorpanakha's husband by mistake. After that, he sent Shoorpanakha to Dandaka Forest. He also sent their mother's younger sister's son Khara with fourteen thousand army men to protect Shoorpanakha.

Ravana next went to Indraloka and challenged the devas to a war with him. Indra commanded the devas to fight with Ravana. Indrajith with the magical power he had received from Brahma, bound Indra and took him captive. Brahma intervened and Indrajith let Indra free. After winning over Indra, he got the name Indrajith meaning the one who won the war with Indra. Brahma also gave him another blessing, "If you do a *homa* and go for battle, you will not be killed by anybody."

Agastya muni also explained how Ravana was overpowered by king of Haihaya named Karthaveeryarjuna. He was released at the request of Pulasthya muni. Ravana after that went to Kishkindha and decided to fight with Vali. Vali was in meditation at that time. Vali understood Ravana had come to fight him. Vali caught him and hung him on his girdle. He flew for a long time above the sea and when he got tired he went to a flower garden and put Ravana down. He asked Ravana to introduce himself. Ravana introduced himself to Vali and they became friends.

Birth of Hanuman and His Blessings

After hearing all this, Rama asked Agastya muni, "My opinion is that Hanuman is stronger than Ravana and Vali. It would have been impossible for me to defeat Ravana without the presence of Hanuman. He is an extremely strong warrior and a selfless person. Why did not Hanuman help Sugreeva in the war between Vali and Sugreeva?"

Agastya muni said, "Hanuman was not aware of his real strength. Now I am going to tell you about Hanuman."

*****

In the Meru Mountain, there was a famous and great monkey named Kesari. His wife Anjana had a son from Vayudeva and he is called Hanuman. When Anjana had gone to the forest to collect fruits and roots, Hanuman was very hungry. He leapt towards the sun, thinking it was a fruit. After seeing Hanuman, his father Vayudeva tried to protect him from the hot sun by blowing a cool breeze. The sun god knew that Hanuman was going to serve Rama in the war and hence did not punish or harm him. That time Rahu came to swallow the sun. After seeing this, the small Hanuman tried to swallow Rahu. Rahu went to Indra for shelter. Indra came on Airavatha to protect Rahu. When Hanuman saw Airavatha, he turned towards it. Indra used the Vajrayudha and Hanuman was struck and fell on a mountain. Vayudeva was very angry, he took the motionless body of Hanuman and stopped the air from moving. Everyone found it difficult to breath and were gasping for breath. All the devas approached Brahma and requested him to help.

Brahma went to Vayu and lovingly moved his hand along Hanuman's head and Hanuman was revived. Brahma requested everybody to bless the child Hanuman because he was going to do a lot of good for human kind. Indra put a lotus flower garland on Hanuman and gave him a blessing that no Vajrayudha could kill him in the future. Since, his cheek was broken during the fall he was named Hanuman. Surya gave a part of his brightness to Hanuman, and also blessed him with good spiritual knowledge and fluency in speaking. Vayu blessed him that he would not die in water. Yama blessed him that time would not affect him and he would never be slain in battle. Kubera gave him a blessing that he would not be killed with a mace or feel tired in a war. Mahadeva gave a blessing that he would not be killed by him or by his arms. Viswakarma gave a blessing that he would not be killed by his arms.

The last blessing was from Brahma. "You will have long life, greatness and ability to withstand the Brahmasthra." Brahma told Vayudeva, "This child will have the ability to change his shape as he wishes. He will not be conquerable by anybody in the war, he can travel at very high speed and to speed up the destruction of Ravana, he will be the favourite of Rama."

After all the devas disappeared, Vayudeva gave Hanuman to his mother Anjana to look after and protect him. Hanuman was a very naughty child. He used to harm the rishis. His foster father Kesari and his father Vayudeva tried to teach him how to behave, but they did not succeed. The rishis therefore cursed him, "You will lose your memory about your strength, and you will remember it only when someone reminds you about it."

After losing the memory about his strength, Hanuman became calm and spent his time wandering in the forests. At that time, the father of Vali and Sugreeva, Riksharaj died due to old age. Vali the eldest son was made the king while Sugreeva was made the prince. Sugreeva and Hanuman were childhood friends. When Vali and Sugreeva became enemies, Hanuman could not help Sugreeva since he had forgotten about his strength. But Hanuman used his talent to acquire spiritual knowledge and became equal to Brihaspathi in his spiritual knowledge.

*****

After Agastya muni had told them all this, Rama told all the rishis to come again for the *yagya* he was going to conduct in the future.

After everyone left, Rama came to the palace after finishing his morning rituals. Rama ruled the country efficiently with the help of ministers, employees, twenty monkey captains, many strong rakshasas and was very happy in their services. Rama went to the houses of King Janaka, his maternal uncle Yudhajith and more than three hundred kings and princes and gave them gifts. Whatever gifts Rama received he gave to Vibheeshana, Sugreeva, the monkey troops and rakshasas.

Rama made Hanuman and Angada sit on his lap and told them, "You both deserve all the honours." He removed all the ornaments he was wearing and gave them to Hanuman and Angada. Rama told all the monkeys, "You are not only my friends but also equal to my brothers."

After that all the monkeys stayed there happily for one month as the guests of Rama. Rama requested Sugreeva to go back to Kishkindha and Vibheeshana to Lanka so that they could rule over their respective kingdoms. Hanuman requested Rama to bless him that his attachment and devotion (*bhakthi*) to him should be everlasting. Rama hugged Hanuman and said, "You will be remembered in the world so long as the story of Ramayana exists in the world. I have nothing with me to compensate you for the help you have rendered to me." Rama then bade farewell to Vibheeshana, Sugreeva and all the monkeys.

One day, Rama heard a voice from the sky. It was the Pushpaka vimana. "As instructed by you, I had gone to Kubera. Kubera told that since you had won the war against Ravana, I should be owned by you."

Rama received the plane, bowed to it and said, "Whenever I require your service, I will call or ask for it." The plane then flew away.

Rama and Seetha lived happily for a few months. Seetha became pregnant during that time. Rama was extremely happy. Rama asked Seetha, "Is there any desire left in your mind which you could not do or accomplish? I am waiting to hear that from you, so that I can help you to accomplish that desire."

Seetha said, "The moment I joined you, all my desires were accomplished. Since you have asked me, I will tell you my desire: I want to visit all rishis staying on the Ganga River shores, touch their feet and bow to them as a mark of respect."

Rama said that her desire would be accomplished.

Rama during this period sent some spies across Ayodhya to find out the opinion of the people about his rule. Most of the houses the spies visited had a very good opinion about Rama and his administration. In the house of a washerman they saw the husband beating his wife. He shouted, "Whom were you sleeping with last night? I will not therefore accept you in my house."

The mother of the washerman told his son not to do so. The washerman became very angry and said, "I am not a great man like Rama who accepted his wife after staying with another man."

The spy got angry after hearing this. He wanted to kill the washerman. But he remembered the instructions given by Rama that nobody should be killed or harmed.

There is a sub story for this. King Janaka brought up Seetha as her own daughter. When she was playing with her playmates, she saw two beautiful love birds. They were talking about Rama and Seetha. According to Seetha's request, the playmates caught these two birds and put them in a cage. The male bird somehow got escaped from there and flew away. The female bird told Seetha that she was pregnant and requested Seetha to release her. Seetha did not agree.

That bird cursed Seetha, "You who have separated me from my beloved, will also be separated by your beloved during your pregnancy." After saying this, the female bird died. The male bird could not bear the sorrow and it jumped in River Ganga. The bird cursed Seetha saying that he would be reborn as a washerman, and be the cause of Seetha getting separated from Rama.

The next day Rama called Bhadra the spy and asked him, "What message do you have for me? What are the opinions the people have about the king?"

Bhadra said that all the people had a very good opinion, except for a washerman who had a different opinion. "Whatever work you have done, like killing Ravana, and construction of bridge Ram Sethu are all praiseworthy. But Seetha stayed with another person which was not acceptable to the washerman. The washerman said, 'Just because Rama accepted Seetha, should the people also do such similar things?'"

Rama was surprised and disturbed to hear this. He sent another spy to find out the truth. They repeated the same thing. Rama became unconscious and fell on the floor.

After he became conscious, he called Bharata and asked, "Should I commit suicide or give up Seetha?" Bharata became very angry. He decided to go and kill the washerman. Rama did not allow that. Bharata reminded Rama about Seetha's loyalty and purity as an individual. Rama said, "Though I have full faith in Seetha, the faith of the people in the king is important to me. I can't lose that. I will therefore give up Seetha. You either cut off my head or take Seetha to a forest and leave her there." Bharata became unconscious after hearing this.

Rama then called Lakshmana and explained everything to him and told him, "I can't let dishonour come to the Ikshwaku family. I have decided to abandon Seetha. You take Seetha tomorrow, and show her all the ashrams on the banks of the Ganga River. She has a desire to visit all the ashrams and show her respect to the rishis by touching their feet. Finally, take her to Valmiki's ashram. My darling brother, please obey what I say and do not hesitate to do this. You will otherwise be subject to my anger."

Lakshmana's heart was broken and he was mentally disturbed. But Lakshmana always implicitly obeyed Rama. He informed Seetha, "Please get ready to go and visit all the ashrams, and to show your respects to the rishis according to your desire. Sumanthra is ready with the chariot."

The next day Seetha happily dressed in silk clothes and special ornaments and said that she would give them as gifts to the rishi's wives. On the way, Seetha told Lakshmana that she was seeing some bad omens. "My right eye is blinking. I feel sad and weak. Is Rama not alright?" Seetha prayed to all the devas for auspicious tidings for Rama and the relatives.

Lakshmana said, "Let no bad things happen to you." They spent that night near the River Gomathi. By noon, they reached the River Ganga. Lakshmana started weeping.

Seetha asked Lakshmana the reason for his sorrow. "Are you not capable of staying away from Rama for two days? We can visit all the rishis, show our respects and go back quickly."

They arranged a boat and they reached the other side of the River Ganga.

Lakshmana said, "I am doing a very sad duty entrusted to me by Rama. I am doing it with a lot of pain and it is not at all justifiable. It would have been better for me to die rather than do this painful and unjustifiable work. You are the most trustworthy loyal wife of Rama. You should excuse me for doing such work." Lakshmana then lay down on the floor and started rolling and crying .

Seetha asked Lakshmana, "Did anything happen to Rama which you find difficult to tell me?"

Lakshmana got up, wiped his tears and explained everything to Seetha. Then he told Seetha. "I know that you are very loyal and lovingly attached to your husband. I do not have any doubts about your integrity. Rama was forced to give you up. Please do not misunderstand him. Do not lose your confidence and courage. Valmiki muni was a very close friend of King Dasaratha. We are going there. You will get love and protection there. Keep your confidence in the muni."

After hearing this, Seetha became unconscious and fell on the floor. She started crying and said, "I have got only bad things in my present life. What sin did I commit? Lakshmana, how will I stay alone in this forest? What will I tell the rishis? I feel like jumping in the River Ganga and committing suicide. But the Ikshwaku family will also die along with me." When she became calmer, she told Lakshmana, "I am not blaming you. You are only obeying the order of the king. Go and tell Rama I was always trustful, loving and devoted to him. My loyalty to him is well known. It was not right on his part to give up me, fearing bad name and shame from the public."

Lakshmana went around Seetha (did *pradakshina),* went inside the boat and travelled to the other side of the river and got into the chariot.

Lakshmana told Sumanthra, "What justification can be there for Rama to treat Seetha in this manner?"

Sumanthra said, "O Lakshmana, all this is destined. Rama is fated to be separated from his loved ones. Once Durvasa muni told Dasaratha about Brighu's curse on Lord Vishnu. Brighu cursed Vishnu that he would be born as a man (Rama) and be separated from his wife."

Some disciples of Valmiki muni saw Seetha. They went running to the muni and said, "A lady looking like Lakshmi Devi is sitting alone and crying in the forest."

Valmiki muni who in advance knew all this with his meditative power went immediately towards Seetha and told her, "O wife of Rama and daughter of King Janaka, leave all your fears. There are female munis in the ashram. They will take care of you like their daughter and protect you. Consider this as your own house." The female munis took Seetha to the ashram.

Lakshmana reached Ayodhya. He saw Rama crying with sorrow and sitting in a very thoughtful mood. He bowed to Rama. He told Rama that he had left Seetha in Valmiki's ashram and said, "In life, we may have to undergo separation from everyone. Do not be sad. You are capable of controlling all three worlds. Can you not control your mind from this sadness? Hearsay and gossip can happen any time from the public."

Rama told Lakshmana to make arrangements to call all the ministers, rishis and public complainants. "Let me start my official duties as a king."

There was no complainant except a dog. Lakshmana asked the dog, "What is the complaint?"

The dog said, "I wish to directly give the complaint to the king. But will you allow a dog to enter the palace? Please go and ask."

Lakshmana told Rama about the dog. Ram told Lakshmana to bring the dog. The dog said, "The king is like God for his people and protector too. The king also ensures justice is there in the country. May I bow to you and say my sad incident to you? A Brahmin hit on my head without me doing any harm to him."

Rama immediately gave orders to summon the Brahmin.

Rama asked the Brahmin, "Why did you hit the dog? What crime has he done?"

Rama said, "Anger destroys all qualities of a man. Intelligent people therefore do not show their anger."

The Brahmin said, "I was going around begging for food. He came in my way. I asked him to give way to me. He refused. I was very hungry and got angry and hit the dog on the head with the stick I had in my hand. You can give any suitable punishment to me. I am ready to accept that."

Rama consulted all the ministers, Agastya muni, Kashyapa muni, and Bhrigu muni and asked their opinion. Their common opinion was not to punish the Brahmin. But they left the final decision to Rama. The dog intervened in between and said, "You had asked me what you should do for me. My desire is that this Brahmin should be made the acharya of Kalanjara ashram." That was accepted by Rama and he did so.

Then Rama said, "You have not really understood the intricacies of karma (work with devotion), but this dog knows about it." Rama asked the dog to give an explanation about what he said.

The dog said, "I was the acharya of Kalanjara ashram in my previous life. I had followed all rules of respecting Brahmins and devas and gave them protection with proper attention. But due to some mistakes in my karma, I was born as a dog in my present life. If an egoistic person takes over the position of acharya, he will destroy himself."

The dog disappeared after saying this. All the people including Rama had the feelings of surprise, fear and respect in their minds after hearing the dog. A person was born as a dog in his next birth due to his egoistic behaviour!

Many rishis had come to see Rama including Chyavana muni and he said, “The son of Madhu, a rakshasa named Lavanasura is doing lot of harm in Madhuvan Forest. Please arrange to kill him and let us live in peace there.”

Shatrughna after hearing agreed to do that duty and told Rama accordingly. Rama crowned Shatrughna as the king of Madhuvan. Shatrughna sent his army to Madhuvan. Shatrughna also started his journey to Madhuvan. On his way, Shatrughna stayed for a day in Valmiki’s ashram. That day Seetha delivered the twin boys, elder one Kusha and the younger one Lava. Shatrughna was very happy to hear this. The next day, Shatrughna reached Madhuvan and killed Lavanasura. He constructed a big city there and stayed there for twelve years. He then returned to Ayodhya. On his way back, he visited Valmiki’s ashram.

Valmiki muni received Shatrughna with due respect. Lava and Kusha were singing songs about Rama’s story with musical instruments. They beautifully described the life of Rama. Shatrughna could not sleep that day. The beautiful words, describing the life of Rama was in his mind. Shatrughna reached Ayodhya, bowed to Rama and said, “I have been staying away from you for the last twelve years. I feel very sad about it. I have constructed a big city in Madhuvan. Can I now stay in Ayodhya?”

Rama told Shatrughna, “A king’s duty is to look after his kingdom. So you must stay in Madhura. You can visit Ayodhya often.”

Ashwamedha Yagya

Rama had a desire to conduct the Rajasuya yagya. Bharata dissuaded him from that.

"All the kings look at you as a father. Do not do such a sacrifice which involves killing many royals. Therefore, it is advisable to conduct the Ashwamedha yaga."

Rama decided to conduct the Ashwamedha yaga. One day, Agastya muni came to the palace to see Rama. During conversation with the muni, Rama told the muni, "I feel guilty of killing Ravana who was the son of a Brahmin. I am ashamed of myself for that act."

Agastya muni told him, "O Rama, you are the protector of the world. You have not sinned in killing Ravana. However, I will tell you a way in which you can remove the sin of killing a Brahmin. You must perform the auspicious horse sacrifice or the Ashwamedha yaga. After worshipping the horse, you must place a note on its forehead with your name. The horse must be let to roam freely, protected by guards. If anyone seizes the horse, the guards should fight him and take back the horse. For two years, you must give alms."

Agastya muni then selected a suitable horse from the stable. It was also decided to conduct the yaga on the banks of the River Sarayu. All the munis like Parvatha, Kapila, Angirass, Vyasa, Athri, Yajnayavalkya and Shuka came for the function. Pavilions were set up for the invited kings. Sugreeva attended on the kings and priests side. There was a splendid royal feast and gold was distributed liberally.

The horse was properly decorated as required by Lakshmana. Shatrughna took the responsibility of protecting the horse. Shatrughna also had the responsibility of defeating the person who tried to tie the horse. Rama sent Pushkala, Bharata's son, along with Shatrughna. Rama gave Pushkala a sword and also allowed Hanuman to accompany them.

The horse roamed through many kingdoms.

The horse then entered the city of Ahichatra. Shatrughna's minister Sumathi informed him that the city was ruled by King

Sumada. Once King Sumada had prayed to Goddess Kamakshi. The goddess was pleased with him and said, "You will be able to destroy your enemies. When Rama performs the horse sacrifice, and the horse enters your kingdom, you must give your kingdom and wealth to Rama."

Sumada on hearing that the horse had entered his kingdom, gave them a kingly reception. Shatrughna and others stayed there for three days.

Then they proceeded. Sumada accompanied them. The horse reached the banks of the Payosni River. There they saw the hermitages of many munis. The horse reached Chyavana muni's ashram. Shatrughna bowed and offered respects to the muni. The muni expressed his desire to see Rama. Shatrughna asked Hanuman to take the muni to Ayodhya.

After staying in Chyavana's ashram for a few days, Shatrughna resumed his journey with the horse. When they reached the Mountain Nila, a prince named Damana saw the horse. There was an instruction written on the horse, "This horse was sent by son of Dasaratha, Rama who can't be conquered. Courageous people can seize the horse. Shatrughna will come and free the horse." Damana, who thought that he could keep the horse with the help of his army, started war against Shatrughna.

Prathapagarya, a king on Shatrughna's side, fought with Damana. Prathapagarya was badly injured in the fight. His army men brought him to a safe place. Bharata then sent Pushkala, his son, to fight. Pushkala injured Damana after a severe battle between them. King Subahu then fought on behalf of Damana. Shatrughna defeated him. King Subahu surrendered and joined Shatrughna in protecting the horse.

One day, the sky became dark and there was lightning and thunder. The horse disappeared. It had been stolen by a rakshasa, Vidyunmali. In a fierce battle that ensued, Shatrughna killed Vidyunmali and recovered the horse.

The sacrificial horse then reached the River Reva. The horse jumped in the river but did not come up. Everybody was afraid. Shatrughna, Hanuman and Pushkala entered the river. There was a big city below the river. They saw a princess surrounded by many beautiful women. The horse was tied to a golden pillar nearby. The women told the princess that she could use the three persons as her food.

The princess saw all three and asked them, "How did you reach here? Even devas find it difficult to reach here. Whoever comes here generally can't go back. Who are you all? Whose horse is this?"

Hanuman said, "We are servants of King Rama. He is conducting the Ashwamedha yaga. Please give us back this horse. If not, we three are capable of killing anyone who refuses to give back the horse."

The princess said, "Nobody can take away the horse I have tied. But I am also a servant of Rama and a devotee of him. I shall therefore give you back the horse. I shall give a boon to please your king."

Hanuman said, "We lack nothing in life due to the blessing of Rama. But give me the blessing that Rama will remain in my mind permanently in all my births."

The princess smiled and said, "It will be so. You will have to face a king named Veeramani who has the blessing of Lord Shiva. I will give you a weapon to face him."

Shatrughna accepted the weapon and started the journey. After travelling for a long distance, they reached a prosperous kingdom called Devapuram. The king of the kingdom was Veeramani and the prince was Rukmangada.

Rukmangada caught the horse and tied it. "Who is this Rama? My father is braver and wealthier than him." Rukmangada reached the palace with the horse. He told his father Veeramani about his capturing the horse. Veeramani was not happy and he felt that his son had acted like a thief. Veeramani took the horse and went to Lord Shiva. Shiva said, "Your son has done the right thing. You know that you have my protection. In this way, we can view Rama's lotus feet."

When the horse was not seen, Shatrughna asked minister Sumathi about the country. Sumathi explained like this, "The king of this country is Veeramani. He has the protection from Lord Siva. We have to therefore make our moves very carefully."

Veeramani had already started preparing for a war. It was suggested that Pushkala would fight first and Shatrughna later. Pushkala first fought with Rukmangada. Pushkala during the battle fired a missile which caused a fire in Rukmangada's chariot and Rukmangada became unconscious. Veeramani came rushing to take revenge.

Veeramani told Pushkala, "You are only a boy. You should not fight with me. I can't be conquered by anybody."

Pushkala replied, "I consider you as an old man. I have defeated your son." In the war that continued, Veeramani became unconscious after getting hit by an arrow from Pushkala.

When the Lord Shiva saw the defeat of his devotee, he sent Veerabhadra to face Pushkala and Nandi to face Hanuman. There was a very big battle between Pushkala and Veerabhadra. Veerabhadra broke Pushkala's chariot. Pushkala came down and they started wrestling. They fought each other, day and night, for four days. On the fifth day Veerabhadra flew up and they started wrestling in the sky. Veerabhadra at last threw Pushkala down on the ground and cut off his head with a thrishul. After that Lord Shiva (Mahadeva) challenged Shatrughna. Shatrughna sent the Brahmasthra, but Mahadeva was untouched by it. Shatrughna became unconscious after getting hit by a fire arrow from the Lord Shiva.

Hanuman on seeing this told Mahadeva, "You are doing injustice. I know that you pray to Rama. I will make you kneel down in the war." Hanuman took a big rock and threw it at Lord

Siva. It hit Mahadeva's chariot and it got damaged. Nandi came running and carried Shiva, his lord, on his shoulder. The arrow sent by Lord Shiva was caught bent, broken and thrown away by Hanuman. Hanuman tied Lord Shiva with his tail and tried to attack him with trees and big stones. Lord Shiva and Nandi were very much surprised to see this.

Lord Shiva then told Hanuman, "You have shown your attacking power in a very wonderful way. I am very happy with you. I am ready to give any blessing that you ask."

Hanuman said, "With the blessings of Rama, I do not lack anything. I am only asking you a favour. I am going to the Mountain Drona to bring the Mritasanjeevani. Pushkala is lying dead and Shatrughna is in an unconscious state. You should protect them. No birds or animals should touch their body till I come."

Mahadev agreed. When Hanuman reached Mountain Drona, he saw devas protecting the mountain. Hanuman defeated all of them. They went and informed Indra. Indra sent some more devas to capture Hanuman. They too were defeated by Hanuman.

Indra went and met their guru Brihaspathi and asked, "Who is Hanuman?"

Brihaspathi said, "He is the devotee of Rama, who is a great warrior who killed Ravana and Kumbhakarna. He has easily set fire to Lanka. He has come here to take medicinal plants to give life to the dead and heal the injured. Give him the permission. Even if you wage war for a hundred years, you will not be able to defeat him." The fear Indra had, went away. Brihaspathi came to Hanuman and asked to forgive them.

After coming back, Hanuman used the medicinal plant on Pushkala's body and prayed to Rama. Pushkala stood up. The first question he asked was, "Where is Veerabhadra?" Hanuman repeated the same method of treatment for Shatrughna. He got up and asked, "Where is Lord Shiva?" Hanuman treated all those who had got injured.

The war started again. Pushkala faced Veerabhadra, Hanuman faced Nandi and Shatrughna faced Lord Shiva in the war. Shatrughna was prevented from going near Lord Shiva by Veeramani. Shatrughna sent a divine arrow at Veeramani. It hit Veeramani on the shoulder and he became unconscious. Mahadeva came to help Veeramani. Shatrughna challenged Mahadeva. A terrible war took place. Shatrughna got tired and worried. Hanuman asked Shatrughna to pray to Rama. He prayed and said, "My dear brother, Lord Shiva is going to take my life in the war. Please protect me." Rama appeared immediately. Shatrughna was surprised. Mahadeva came and touched Rama's feet and bowed to him and said, "I have come to the war to defend my devotees." He also instructed Veeramani to give back the horse.

Rama justified Mahadeva's actions and said that Mahadeva was right in defending his devotees and it is the duty of all devas. Rama also said, "You are in my heart and I am in your heart also. There is no any difference between us. Only bad and cruel minded people find difference between us." Rama touched Veeramani and he became totally well and healthy. Veeramani gave the horse back.

He decided to go with Shatrughna to protect the horse. The sacrificial horse resumed its journey. After travelling for a long time the horse suddenly stopped still like a statue, without any movement. Even after Hanuman tried to dragged the horse, it did not move. Shatrughna asked his minister Sumathi for advice. Sumathi said, "It appears as though we are in the presence of some powerful sage." They then saw an ashram at a distance which belonged to Shaunaka muni. The muni received them graciously. Shatrughna, Hanuman and Pushkala bowed to the muni. While conversing with the muni, they asked him about the horse. Shatrughna said, "Our horse is not able to move. What could be the reason for that?"

Shaunaka spent some time in meditation and said, "The cause for this could be Sathwika muni. He was meditating on the banks of the Kaveri. While undergoing severe penance, he lost his life. He then went to the Mountain Meru. The muni spent his time with apsaras happily below the jambuka tree on the banks of the River Jambavathi. Once, he behaved arrogantly to the apsaras. The munis who saw this cursed him and he became a rakshasa. They told him, 'When you make Rama's horse immobile, you will get a chance to hear stories of Rama. When you hear that you will be blessed and come back to your original state.'"

Shaunaka muni then told Shatrughna to go near the horse and narrate the stories of Rama. He did so. The muni who heard the stories got blessed and rose to the sky and went to heaven. The horse started moving.

The journey continued for seven more months. The horse reached the kingdom of King Suratha. Suratha was a devotee of Rama. Knowing everything, he caught and tied the horse. He did it with the hope that he would have the good luck of seeing Rama personally. Shatrughna asked Sumathi about this king. Sumathi said, "He is a devotee of Rama. We can send Angada as a messenger to him."

Angada went to Suratha's palace and advised Suratha to free and give back the horse. Suratha was not prepared for that. He said that he would release the horse only if Rama came there. "I can defeat all of you very easily."

Then Angada told him, "I feel that you know nothing about Bharata's son Pushkala, Rama's brother Shatrughna and the brave Hanuman. Shatrughna has killed Lavana asura and Vidyunmali. Pushkala pleased even Veerabhadra with his valour. Hanuman killed Ravana's son Aksha. Due to your old age, understanding has left you. Compared to them, you are only a mosquito."

Angada returned and told everything to Shatrughna. A big war broke out between Shatrughna and Suratha. The initial fight was between Suratha's son Champaka and Pushkala. Champaka sent the Ramasthra at Pushkala. He bound Pushkala, and took him in his chariot. Shatrughna sent Hanuman to rescue Pushkala from Champaka. Hanuman and Champaka fought fiercely. Champaka caught Hanuman by the tail, whirled him and threw him. Hanuman just laughed, picked up Champaka by his leg, and threw him to the ground. Champaka became unconscious. Hanuman then rescued Pushkala.

The angry Suratha started fighting with Hanuman. The arrows sent by Suratha was caught, broken and thrown away by Hanuman. Then Hanuman broke eighty bows of the king. Hanuman took the chariot along with Suratha and walked towards the seashore. Suratha hit Hanuman with his mace. Hanuman put the chariot down and destroyed it. Hanuman thus destroyed forty-nine chariots. Suratha next sent the arrow given to him by Mahadeva called Pashupadasthra. That arrow tied Hanuman. He prayed to Rama and got released from that knot. Suratha next prayed to Rama and sent the arrow. Hanuman did not try to get away or avoid the arrow due to his devotion to Rama.

Pushkala then came and started war with Suratha. A big battle took place. Pushkala and Shatrughna fell unconscious after facing Suratha's arrows. Suratha next caught Sugreeva and bound him using the Ramasthra. Suratha told Hanuman, "Pray to Rama and call him here. If he comes, you will be free."

Hanuman then prayed to Rama that he was bound by Suratha and in his custody. Rama and Lakshmana reached there within a short period. Suratha knelt down before Rama and bowed to him. Rama hugged Suratha. Suratha freed everybody and also released the sacrificial horse. Rama blessed all his devotees. All the army men who were unconscious became conscious and got up. They all stayed in Suratha's palace for three days. Rama went back to Ayodhya in the Pushpaka vimana.

Suratha gave the administrative responsibility to Champaka, his son and the prince, and accompanied Shatrughna to protect the sacrificial horse. The horse reached a place where Lava was collecting firewood along with the munis. Lava read what was written on the horse. He asked, "Who is the Kshatriya challenger? Who are Rama and Shatrughna?"

Lava then caught and tied the horse. Those men who were protecting the horse were sent back by Lava with his arrows. They went and informed Shatrughna about the incident. They said that the boy who tied the horse had a face resembling that of Rama when he was a child. Shatrughna sent his warrior Kalajith with the army to release the horse. Kalajith challenged Lava. Lava cut off Kalajith's head with a sword. All the men ran away in fear. Shatrughna next sent Pushkala to get the horse released. A big war took place. In the war, Pushkala became unconscious after getting struck on the shoulder with an arrow sent by Lava. The next person came to face Lava was Hanuman. Hanuman knew that it was impossible to conquer or defeat Lava. Hanuman therefore pretended to be unconscious and fell to the ground.

The next was Shatrughna. When he saw Lava, he remembered the face of Rama when he was young. Lava knocked Shatrughna unconscious using his arrows. When Shatrughna regained his consciousness, he resumed the battle with Lava. Lava thought that this situation would not have arisen if Kusha was with him. Shatrughna sent a blazing arrow at Lava. It hit Lava on his chest and he became unconscious. Shatrughna took the unconscious Lava in his chariot and went away.

The disciples of Valmiki had seen all this. They went and informed Seetha about all these incidents. After hearing this, Seetha started crying and fell unconscious on the ground. Kusha who had gone with the rishis for a pilgrimage returned and came to know all about what had happened in his absence. He went to face the enemies. First he knocked Shatrughna unconscious by striking him with his arrows. He then knocked Hanuman to the ground using a missile. He tied Sugreeva with the Varuna asthra. After that, he tied Hanuman and Sugreeva together and dragged them to the ashram. Seetha was surprised to see all this. Seetha recognised Hanuman and Sugreeva.

Seetha advised the children, “Rama is your father. You have therefore no right or power to catch and tie the sacrificial horse.”

Lava and Kusha said, “A Kshatriya who goes for a war with their guru or father does not commit any sin. However, we will obey your order.”

They released Hanuman and Sugreeva. Seetha prayed to Rama and requested him to heal Shatrughna. The prayer found result and Shatrughna became alright. Sumathi then reminded Shatrughna that the time had come for them to return to Ayodhya. They all returned to Ayodhya.

Rama had got the information from his messengers about the return of the Ashwamedha yagya party. He gave the responsibility to Lakshmana to give a fitting reception to the party. Shatrughna and Pushkala fell at Rama’s feet and bowed to him. Rama lovingly hugged both of them. Sumathi described to Rama all the details about the Ashwamedha yaga. After hearing everything Rama understood that the two boys who were in the ashram were his sons. Rama approached Valmiki muni and enquired about these boys.

Valmiki muni said, “How do you, who knows everything that happens in the three worlds, not know about them?” Valmiki explained to Rama all what had happened after Lakshmana left Seetha in the ashram. He also explained about his writing the Ramayana in the musical form and how Lava and Kusha had learnt that. Rama requested Valmiki to bring Seetha to Ayodhya.

After the yaga was over Rama took the sword given by Agastya muni and tried to cut off its neck, but the moment it touched the head of the horse, the horse took the form of a divine person who got into a chariot and said, “I was a Brahmin in my previous birth but did many injustices and started cheating the people by conducting hollow spiritual practices. Durvasa muni cursed me to be an animal. I fell at the muni’s feet and requested him to forgive him. But the muni said that I would become a sacrificial horse in my next birth and when the sword of Rama touched my neck, I would regain my original form." The divine person disappeared after saying this.

Valmiki called Lava and Kusha and instructed them, "From tomorrow, both of you should start travelling, and sing Ramayana songs around the world to propagate Rama's story. You should do it in cities, ashrams and houses. Let it be heard by all. First go to Ayodhya. If you get an invitation to sing songs of Ramayana in the palace in presence of Brahmins, do it. But do not accept any gifts given by Rama. Tell him that you are used to eating simple food like fruits and roots and do not have any requirements for gold. If Rama asks whose children you are, tell him you are the disciples of Valmiki muni."

After listening to everything that Valmiki said, they agreed. "We are ready for it and will do as you have suggested."

The next day, Lava and Kusha took the musical instruments in their hands and started their journey to Ayodhya. They sang the Ramayana epic all along the way. Their music was very beautiful to hear. It was better than the music of gandharvas. They wore clothes made of deerskin. They finally reached Rama's palace and sang their songs. Rama asked Lakshmana to give the boys twenty thousand gold coins and dresses.

The boys refused to accept them and said, "Our food is fruits and roots and therefore why would we require gold?"

Rama asked, "Dear boys, how many chapters are there in this story? Who wrote this epic?"

They answered, "O great king, it was authored by Valmiki muni. It had six chapters and the seventh one also was added later. If you desire, we will complete all."

Rama listened very happily. Rama then thought that these twin sons could be Seetha's sons. Rama's mind and heart was full of love and affection for his sons.

Seetha Vanishing into the Earth

Rama sent a messenger to Valmiki muni. The messenger said, "If Seetha is virtuous, let her come here and prove it in front of the public. She should come with the permission of Valmiki."

Seetha was very unhappy with the suggestion of Rama. She felt that public questioning was not right. But she took a decision in her mind and started her journey to Ayodhya with Valmiki muni. She had already proved her virtues in front of all the devas and rishis. She walked with Valmiki with folded hands and bowed head. They reached Ayodhya.

Valmiki told Rama, "O son of Dasaratha, here stands your wife who is very virtuous with the best mind whom you gave up, fearing bad name from the public. She is prepared to prove her virtues. Please give your command." Valmiki continued, "If Seetha has an iota of bad virtue, let all that I have gained by my meditation disappear. Despite fully knowing that she is virtuous, you gave her up cruelly fearing bad name from the public."

After hearing this, Rama said, "I accept whatever you told me is true and fully correct. Despite that, the people spoke badly about me. I had to give her up with a lot of agony. If she can prove her virtues now in front of the people, I am prepared to accept her as my beloved wife."

All were silent and looked at Seetha. With her head down and looking down, she spoke very clearly and legibly, "Bhumidevi, please listen to my request. If I am true, please protect me from these people and their false accusations."

When Seetha was speaking these words, the earth started to split. Bhumidevi dressed royally came up in a divine chariot. She hugged Seetha, made her sit by her side and disappeared and vanished below the earth.

The spectators were silent. All started praising Seetha. She had proved her good loyalty and virtues. People were not fully satisfied even after praising her and her virtues. The devas and devis appeared in the sky and showered flowers. Tears started flowing from Rama's eyes. He got angry and demanded Bhumidevi to give him Seetha back. "If Seetha is your daughter, I am your son-in-law. Please also take me along with Seetha. If you do not do that, I will destroy all the mountains on earth and also all the forests."

Brahma came and told Rama, "O Lord, you know who you are, you are Lord Vishnu. Seetha Devi is the sign of prosperity, Lakshmi Devi. Devi is now in the snake's world. When the time comes, she will join you in Vaikunda. O lord of the universe, you who keeps everything in proper order in the universe need not be told about yourself. Listen to the remaining part of the Ramayana from your sons. Ramayana will exist in the world as long as the world exists."

Rama along with Lava and Kusha reached Valmiki's ashram. He invited all the rishis and requested Lava and Kusha to start singing the Uthara kanda of the Ramayana. They then returned to Ayodhya. Despite all these trials, Rama ruled the country with equality and justice to the people. The country prospered. After a few more years, Koushalya, Sumithra and Kaikeyi passed away. The king of Kekaya, Yudhajith came and requested Rama to defeat the king of Gandharva, Syloosha and annexe the country with Ayodhya. Rama announced Bharata's sons Thaksha and Pushkala the princes of that country and they were crowned. Bharata went to Gandharva and defeated King Syloosha in the war. Bharata made Thaksha the king of Thakshashila and Pushkala the king of Pushkalavathi and crowned them with proper rituals. Bharata remained there for five years and then returned to Ayodhya. Rama crowned Lakshmana's sons Angada and Chithrakethu as the kings of Karupatha. Lakshmana remained there for one year giving necessary instructions to them in administration. He then returned to Ayodhya.

The End of Rama's Life on Earth

The time had arrived for Rama to end his life period on earth. Kalamoorthi came as a sanyasi to Rama's palace gate and told Lakshmana that he was a messenger of Brahma and had come with a very important mission. "I have to see Rama immediately."

Kalamoorthi was seated on a golden chair in the palace by Rama. Rama asked him, "What is your intention of coming here? What message do you have for me?"

The messenger replied, "The message to you by Brahma is very secretive in nature. Nobody should hear this. The person who hears this will get the punishment of death. You will have to disown that person."

Rama agreed to that. He told Lakshmana to send the watchman away because the meeting was very secretive. He asked him to stand guard.

When they were alone, Kalamoorthi as the messenger told the message, "As per our request, you were born on the earth to reduce the difficulties people faced by the cruel rakshasas. You have killed Ravana and ruled the country for many years. Now as per your wish you can go back to your original place." Rama said, "You have done your duty as a messenger. I wish you all the best in your life. Please tell Brahma that I have completed all duties that the devas wanted me to do. I will therefore go back to my divine home."

During this secret meeting, Durvasa muni came and stood near the palace gate. He told Lakshmana that he wanted to meet Rama immediately. "I have come for a very essential work and need see Rama immediately." Lakshmana told Durvasa muni to be patient and wait for some time and that Rama had instructed him not to allow anybody to come inside. Durvasa got angry. He told Lakshmana, "Go and inform him of my presence here. If you disobey me, I will destroy the Ikshwaku family. Inform Rama immediately."

Lakshmana knew that if he did any obstruction to the secretive meeting, he would have to face the death penalty. But he decided that it was better to die rather than suffer the anger of Durvasa muni. Lakshmana entered the room and informed Rama about the arrival of Durvasa muni.

Rama bid farewell to Kalamoorthi and came and met Durvasa muni with folded hands. He asked, "What is your need now?"

Durvasa muni said, "I was in meditation for many years. What arrangement will you make for my food?" Rama immediately arranged a very good feast for Durvasa muni. He was happy.

After Durvasa muni left, Rama thought about the words told by Kalamoorthi. His heart started beating fast. The thought that he would lose his brother as per the words of Kalamoorthi made Rama very sad. Rama called all his ministers, explained to them all the incidents and asked for their advice.

Vasishta muni told Rama, "I had seen with my divine power all that had happened to you. Now the only way left is to give justice the first priority. Please therefore send Lakshmana out of the country."

Rama was in very thoughtful mood for some time. He then gave the instruction to send Lakshmana out of the country to keep justice. All the ministers praised the decision taken by Rama. Lakshmana went and sat on the banks of the Sarayu. He started meditation. Indra came there with a divine chariot and took

Lakshmana bodily to heaven. Rama after that decided to give the country to Bharata. Bharata was not ready for that. The country was therefore divided into two parts. The north part was given to Kusha and the south part was given to Lava. The crowning functions of both the sons as kings were also conducted as per the customary rituals. Rama hugged his two sons and blessed them.

Rama then started for his Vanaprastha. There are four phases in the Hindu way of life. They are Brahmacharyashrama which means education period, Grihasthashrama which means living as a family man, Vanaprasthashrama, which means giving up everything and going to the forest and fourth Sanyasashrama which means become a sanyasi. Bharata and Shatrughna also accompanied him. All the people accompanied them, with love and regards.

Ayodhya became empty and deserted without people. Rama was found to be without any emotions and without any attachment to the beloved ones. It was the face of someone ready to leave the world. Shreedevi, Bhumidevi, Shakthi, Oomkara, Gayathri and Vedas had accompanied him. Bharata and Shatrughna along with the family members also had accompanied him.

They reached the River Sarayu. Brahma with divine chariots and divine devas were seen in the sky. Gandharvas and apsaras were singing and dancing. Flowers were showered from the heaven. Rama after some time entered the river and stood in the water.

Brahma praised Rama, "O Lord, as a divine person born in the Raghu family you have completed the purpose of your birth. You are in the process of going to heaven. You are cause of everything on earth, all the living beings on earth depend on you. You are the cause of existence of the whole universe, and the starting point of all lives and things without life. Please therefore accept our thanks, love and warm regards. *Pranam, Pranam, Pranam.*" (Pranam means bowing head down with respect.)

After that Rama, Bharata and Shatrughna entered in the waters of the Sarayu and went to their heavenly abode.

END OF RAMAYANA